Collins | Plays Plus

The Tulip Touch

by

Anne Fine

based on her novel
The Tulip Touch

Resource Material
Rachel O'Neill

Series Consultant
Cecily O'Neill

Published by Collins Educational, an imprint of HarperCollins*Publishers* Ltd, 77–85 Fulham Palace Road, London W6 8JB

| www.**Collins**Education.com |
| On-line support for schools and colleges |

© 2002 playscript Anne fine, resource material Rachel O'Neill

First published 2002.   10 9 8 7 6 5 4 3 2

ISBN 000 713 0864

Based on the novel *The Tulip Touch*, first published by Hamish Hamilton Ltd in 1996, published in paperback by Puffin Books (ISBN 014 037 808 1).

Anne Fine asserts the moral right to be identified as the author of the playscript; Rachel O'Neill asserts the moral right to be identified as the author of the resource material.

British Library Cataloguing in Publication Data

A catalogue record for this book is available from the British Library.

Acknowledgements

The following permissions to reproduce material are gratefully acknowledged:

Illustrations: p79, Photofusion; p91, Stone.

Text: extract from novel of *The Tulip Touch* by Anne Fine is reproduced with permission of Hamish Hamilton Ltd, p75; extract from *Cat's Eye* by Margaret Atwood is reproduced with permission of Bloomsbury Publishing plc, pp83-85; extract from 'Billy Liar' is reproduced by permission of The Agency (London) Ltd © Waterhall Production's Ltd 1960, First published by Evan's Plays, pp87-90; extract from *The Orchard on Fire* by Sheena Mackay, published by William Heinemann. Reprinted with permission of The Random House Group Ltd, pp93-94; extract from *Once in a House on Fire* by Andrea Ashworth is reproduced with permission of Macmillan.

Whilst every effort has been made to contact the copyright holders, this has not proved possible in every case.

Design by Nigel Jordan
Cover design by Nigel Jordan
Cover photograph by Stone
Commissioning Editor: Helen Clark
Editors: Charlie Evans, Gavin Jones

Production: Katie Morris
Typeset by Jordan Publishing Design, Salisbury
Printed And Bound In Thailand By Imago

For permission to perform this play, please allow plenty of time and contact: Permissions Department, HarperCollins*Publishers*, 77–85 Fulham Palace Road, London W6 8JB. Tel. 0181 741 7070.

| You might also like to visit |
| www.**fire**and**water**.co.uk |
| The book lover's website |

Contents

KEY

 cross-reference between playscript and teaching resources.

Background to the play

The Tulip Touch is a story about a friendship that goes horribly awry.

Natalie might live in "The Palace", but, endlessly surrounded by guests, and forced to be on her best behaviour, her home life isn't quite real. And, in a busy hotel, it isn't easy to get attention if you're not paying for it – especially when your younger brother is the family favourite.

Tulip's home life is horrible. No wonder she prefers to spend her days in what, for her, is an enchanting world of plush rooms, rich carpets, curving staircases and hidden gardens. The two girls' needs interlock. Tulip provides the wild, imaginative games, and Natalie has someone to be with and follow.

But Tulip's not just clever and inventive, with her wild lies, her sinister games, and her worrying depths of experience and knowledge. She's mean and spiteful, too. She takes pleasure in hurting. It gives her a sense of power to make her 'enemies' cry, and as she gets older, she plays her games even more viciously.

Born evil? Or simply hardened off too young? After all, as Mr Barnes says, she's had such a rotten start, it's hardly surprising she's so insensitive to other people's feelings. Her father is so vindictive and wilful, it must seem she gets in trouble whatever she does. So why bother?

In the novel on which this play is based, the point is made that, in Tulip's eyes as well, it was the world around her that was wrong. If that had only been arranged more fairly and kindly, then she would never have had to lie or steal, or be spiteful. She'd be a nice, good person – "the girl she was inside, before it all went wrong and she got spoiled all along with it".

Inside the play, we explore the old, old question: nature, or nurture? Good parenting is the hardest job. When it goes wrong, everyone suffers. So why do things have to sink as far as desperate before help comes? We know the problem, so why have we still not bothered to create a society that catches the unfortunate as they fall, and holds them up, to make the world not only better for them but safer for everyone?

Perhaps because, all around us, we see the people who have managed to do it alone – who have risen like phoenixes from difficult beginnings. People can choose to make good. The harsher the start, the harder it is. But it can always be done. It is never too late.

In the end, Natalie will have to make a decision. We've all had friends we've wanted to leave behind. Maybe we've changed, and they haven't. Perhaps they've spent so much time acting up, smashing things, or spoiling their own, or other people's chances, that we got fed up and wanted to spend our time with someone else, or doing something different.

It takes true grit to break away and stay away, and spend your lonely hours reaching for something that will, in the end, be richer and better than the thrills people like Tulip have on offer.

But suppose the other person sees what's happening, and doesn't want to let go...

Awards

The novel of *The Tulip Touch* has won the following awards in the UK:

- Winner of the Whitbread Children's Book Award, 1996

- Highly Commended, Carnegie Medal, 1997

- Shortlisted for the Sheffield Children's Book Award, 1997

- Wirral Paperback of the Year 1998

- Runner-up for Lancashire Library Children's Book of the Year

In the US:

- American Library Association Notable Children's Book

- Booklist Editor's Choice 'Top of the List' Fiction

- Bulletin, Blue Ribbon List 1997

- School Library Journal's Best Books of 1997

- River Bank Review, Children's Book of Distinction.

Characters

TULIP PIERCE Imaginative, bright, tense and excitable. Throughout the time period of the play, the tensions from her home life cause her to be increasingly tempestuous and 'disturbed'. She has a volcanic personality. When things burst through, she can't control them.

THE BARNES FAMILY

NATALIE BARNES A rather subdued girl, and a born follower. She's slightly jealous of her mother's concern for her younger brother. She loves her father. But the only person who can really animate her is Tulip.

MR BARNES An excellent hotelier, and, though he means well, he is too busy to be as good a father as he might be. He has a soft spot for Tulip, recognising how much of her personality and behaviour stems from her difficult background.

MRS BARNES Forever busy, forever distracted, the only thing that ever truly catches overworked Mrs Barnes' attention is her precious Julius.

JULIUS BARNES He has not asked for all this attention. It just comes. And, well aware of the unfairness of it, he treats his elder sister Natalie with special generosity.

HOTEL GUESTS

MR SCOTT-HENDERSON Silver-haired and ageing, Mr Scott-Henderson is still clever, observant and open. More than a little bored by his life of retirement, he takes a particular interest in everyone and everything around him.

Mrs Pettifer A kind and motherly widow. She tries to think well of everyone, and it's a bit of a mystery how she gets on so well with her more acid friend Miss Ferguson.

Miss Ferguson Sharp-eyed, sharp-tongued, and a little too quick to put the least generous interpretation on everyone's behaviour.

OTHER CHARACTERS

Mrs Golightly The head teacher.

Police officers 1 and 2 one male, one female.

Mrs Stoddart A guest at the hotel.

Cecily Mrs Stoddart's daughter.

Old Man

Teacher

Mrs Bodell

Other school pupils, in particular **Marcie, Jamie, Andrew, Glenys, Megan, Josh**.

Various hotel staff and guests.

The Tulip Touch

ACT ONE
Scene One

The action takes place in The Palace – a splendid, if faded, old country house hotel with a grand verandah, a sweeping staircase and stone steps down to fine gardens. As Natalie introduces the story, everyone on stage is silently and unobtrusively reading newspapers, sipping drinks, studying paperwork, etc, until suddenly they are galvanised into more bustling life. From time to time, various differing guests crossing the public rooms, waiting on sofas, or dropping keys off at reception, etc, give the impression of a quiet and well-heeled, gradually changing clientele.

NATALIE Meet everyone. That's Mr Scott-Henderson. He practically lives here. I'm not even sure he's got another home. These are Miss Ferguson and Mrs Pettifer. They're practically fixtures as well. I don't know those guests over there. They only checked in this morning. Here is my Dad.

MR BARNES *on the telephone* A south-facing double room. Yes, indeed. And dinner on both evenings. Thursday and Friday next.

NATALIE That is my Mum.

MRS BARNES *leaning over the main bannister* Natalie! I know I promised I'd take you into town this afternoon. But we've just hit a problem with the laundry, and I promised I'd drop Julius off for a swim. You don't mind, do you, sweet?

*Not even waiting for an answer, **Mrs Barnes** turns back to the housemaid.*

NATALIE This is my brother Julius. He's my Mum's favourite. He always has been and he always will be.

*Julius picks up the dish of peppermints from the reception desk as he passes and offers it to **Natalie**.*

Julius *apologetically* You could come swimming too, Nat.

Natalie It's OK. It doesn't matter.

Julius Well, if you're **sure**...

Natalie No, really. Don't worry. I wasn't really expecting her to have the time to do what **both** of us want. Honestly. *(Julius wanders off, shrugging)* And here's where we live. The Palace. Really. That's what it's called. It's been a hotel for a hundred years. It sits on its lawns like a giant great wedding cake set out on a perfect green tablecloth. It has sixty-three bedrooms, and forty more rooms on top of that, if, as well as the lounges and dining rooms and bars, you count attics and cellars. I've loved it from the moment we came.

Natalie does a cartwheel.

Mrs Pettifer Happy, dear?

Miss Ferguson When isn't she?

Mrs Pettifer That's true enough. How long have I been coming? Five years? And whenever I've looked at the child, she's been somersaulting down the lawns, and balancing along the verandah edges–

Miss Ferguson *reprovingly* And bouncing on the sofas.

Natalie That's only when I was little.

Mrs Pettifer And cartwheeling all the way across the ballroom.

Miss Ferguson *still critical* And throwing apples at the statue in the lily pond.

Natalie Only windfalls.

Mrs Pettifer And creeping after the peacocks.

Miss Ferguson And hiding in the stone urns on the terrace to listen to people's private conversations.

Mrs Pettifer No. To be fair, that's Tulip.

Miss Ferguson *sighing and shaking her head* Ah. Tulip!

NATALIE Ah, Tulip. That's who I'm waiting for. I'll tell you how we met. Years ago.

Natalie slaps a sunhat on her head, and appears younger. **Mr Barnes** *loosens his tie and comes to hold her hand. Together, they walk into:*

Scene Two

A cornfield in high summer.

MR BARNES Stick to the sides, Nat. I don't fancy getting in a tangle with the neighbours about damaging their corn.

NATALIE *pointing* What's that? In the middle of the field. Is it a scarecrow?

MR BARNES *shading his eyes* Is it? No. Surely not. It's moving. You know, I do believe that it's a little girl!

NATALIE What is she doing out here, all alone?

MR BARNES Let's ask. He-llooo! Hell-oooo!

Tulip comes slowly towards them.

NATALIE She's holding something.

MR BARNES That's right. She looks as if she's cuddling something really precious.

NATALIE *thrilled* It's a kitten!

Natalie rushes towards **Tulip.**

MR BARNES Natalie! Be careful! Mind the crop!

Natalie stops. **Tulip** *continues to pick her way through the corn towards them.*

NATALIE *reaching out to stroke the kitten* Oh, it's beautiful. What's its name? What are you going to call it?

MR BARNES It would be more polite, Natalie, to ask the young lady her name first. *(Tulip just stares)* Well, I'll start. I'm Mr Barnes, from the hotel. The Palace. We took it over just a couple of weeks ago. And this is Natalie.

TULIP Tulip.

NATALIE The kitten?

TULIP No. Me.

NATALIE Tulip? Is that really your name? Tulip?

MR BARNES And are you lost, dear?

TULIP Lost?

MR BARNES Well, wandering about, so far from home…

TULIP I live here. This is my dad's field.

MR BARNES You're Mr Pierce's daughter?

TULIP Yes.

MR BARNES *uneasily* Well, Natalie. Probably time to be getting back now. Say goodbye.

NATALIE But we've only just –

MR BARNES *firmly* Come along, Nat. Well, goodbye, Tulip. It was very nice to meet you – and your kitten.

NATALIE Yes. *(Mr Barnes takes Natalie's hand. Natalie breaks away and runs back. She gabbles from nerves)* Tulip, I know this is stupid, because we've only just come to live here, and I don't even know you. But I've hardly met anyone yet. And – well – do you want to be **friends?** *(Tulip just smiles. Mr Barnes and Natalie walk out of earshot)* How did you **know?**

MR BARNES Know what?

NATALIE That she was called Pierce. How did you **know** that?

MR BARNES *uneasily* Oh, just from some gossip I overheard in one of the bars, I expect.

NATALIE But, to remember! Anyway, can I go?

MR BARNES Go?

NATALIE To her house. To their farm. To visit her.

MR BARNES *turning to face her* Now listen, Natalie. I want this clearly understood, right from the start. You are not going over to Tulip's house. She can come to The Palace as often as she likes. But you're not going there. So, if I were you, I'd make some other friends as soon as you start at your new school.

NATALIE But –

MR BARNES I'm not going to discuss it, Natalie. You're not to go there. Ever. And that is final.

Scene Three

In The Palace. From time to time, chefs, housemaids, etc, cross behind. At the reception desk, **Mrs Barnes** *answers phone calls and responds to guests' queries.* **Natalie** *is playing cat's cradles on the verandah, beside* **Mr Scott-Henderson,** *who is sipping a gin and tonic. Sighing, she throws the string down.*

MRS BARNES *looking up briefly* If you're bored, play with Julius.

NATALIE *scowling* I'm not **that** bored.

MRS BARNES You **look** that bored. You **act** that bored.

NATALIE I'm waiting for Tulip.

MR SCOTT-HENDERSON What sort of magic does she have for you? You've got a whole world here. Lawns, potting sheds, shrubberies, terrace gardens. Not to mention a thousand games and amusements left by people who don't leave enough time to pack their children's stuff up properly. And yet, whenever I look at you, you're 'waiting for Tulip'.

NATALIE There she is! Tulip! Tulip! I've been **waiting.** *(Tulip strolls in)* What do you want to play with? Those pogo sticks we found in the attics? Or that funny old flower press? Or the kites? Yes. The kites!

TULIP *licking a finger and raising it* Not enough wind.

*Mr Barnes comes in with a pile of newspapers and hands one to **Mr Scott-Henderson.***

MR BARNES Flying kites, eh? At least that'll be quiet. What was
that game you two were playing yesterday, when Miss Ferguson
complained about the noise?

TULIP 'Rats in a Firestorm'.

MR BARNES Did you find somewhere more sensible to play it?

TULIP We moved down to the cellars, and called it 'Hogs in a
Tunnel' instead.

MR BARNES Very pleasant! Though I suppose it's still less of a
bother than that game you were playing all last week.

TULIP Which? 'Fat in the Fire'?

NATALIE It was 'Malaria!' most of last week.

MR SCOTT-HENDERSON Why don't you invent some quiet games?

NATALIE I don't invent them. Tulip invents the games.

MR BARNES So? How about it, Tulip?

TULIP There's 'Road of Bones'. That's very quiet. And we play 'Days
of Dumbness' quite a lot. No noise at all in that one.

MR BARNES *shuddering* 'Days of Dumbness'! 'Road of Bones'! Don't
the two of you ever play anything pleasant?

TULIP *grinning* I suppose you played things like 'Happy Families'
and 'Tickle the Baby' when you were young.

MR SCOTT-HENDERSON Yes. That's the sort of thing we used to play
back in the good old days.

TULIP What's the worst thing you ever did, Mr Barnes?

MR BARNES When I was a child? *(thoughtfully)* I suppose the thing I
feel worst about, even after all this time, was dropping my
grandfather's tortoise on the garden path. I didn't have the guts

13

to go and tell, so I just shoved it out of sight under the nearest bush.

TULIP *eyes gleaming* Did it **smash?**

MR BARNES *frostily* Its shell did crack, yes.

TULIP Was it an accident?

MR BARNES *sharply* Of **course** it was an accident! You don't suppose I **threw** it?

TULIP No. *(after a pause)* You should have put it in the freezer, of course.

MR BARNES *astonished* In the **freezer?**

TULIP To kill it. It's the kindest way, for fish and terrapins. Probably for tortoises as well.

MR BARNES Tulip, how would you ever know that?

TULIP *casually* I suppose I just heard it somewhere. And remembered it.

MR BARNES *carefully* And do the things you hear worry you?

TULIP No. Sometimes I think about them for a bit. But mostly I'm interested more than I'm worried.

NATALIE Oh, come on, Tulip. Let's go up to the attics to get the dress-ups. We could do a play!

TULIP All right. You can be – oh, look! The gardener's carrying more stuff round behind the rose garden. Perhaps he's going to have another bonfire. *(racing off)* Come on, Natalie! A bonfire!

NATALIE Tulip, we watched his last bonfire. And the one before that. And they're so boring!

MR BARNES Too late, Nat. She's gone.

MR SCOTT-HENDERSON Is that Tulip off to worship the fire gods again? I thought you two were going to root out the dress-ups and put on a play.

NATALIE *bitterly* We were.

*Natalie trudges off after **Tulip**.*

MR SCOTT-HENDERSON She's a strange one, that Tulip.

Natalie stops, out of sight, to eavesdrop.

MR BARNES Hardly surprising, given her father's reputation.

MR SCOTT-HENDERSON Oh, he's a mean piece of work.

*In walk **Mrs Pettifer** and **Miss Ferguson**.*

MRS PETTIFER Where's Tulip off to in such a hurry? The child practically bowled us both over.

MR SCOTT-HENDERSON Gone to watch the bonfire.

MRS PETTIFER She is a weird one. Do you know, after Julius's birthday, I came through the writing room on my way in to dinner and Tulip was sitting in the grate like Little Polly Flinders, tearing all the leftover fancy wrapping paper into strips and dropping them, one by one, into the fire. I said to her, 'It flares up in such pretty colours, doesn't it?' And, do you know, she was quite fierce with me. 'Not just pretty!' she practically snapped at me. 'Magic!'

MISS FERGUSON Not the best manners.

MRS PETTIFER Not the best upbringing. Poor little mite!

MISS FERGUSON Poor little mite indeed! I reckon some mean thoughts go on behind those pretty smiles of hers.

MR SCOTT-HENDERSON And she certainly tells some whoppers.

MR BARNES *laughing* Doesn't she just? And they've all got that little Tulip touch.

MRS PETTIFER Tulip touch?

MR BARNES You know. That tiny detail that almost makes you wonder if, just this once, she might be telling the truth.

MRS PETTIFER You're right! Last week she told me she'd just seen some man in the street keel over, and had phoned for an ambulance. I didn't for a moment believe her because I'd been on the High Street all that time and I hadn't heard any sirens. And then she said, 'And while he was lying there, his fingers kept twitching, so his wedding ring made a little pinging noise against the metal of the drain in the gutter.' And I thought, 'No one makes that sort of tiny detail up. So it must be true.'

MR BARNES No. That's it. That's the Tulip touch.

MR SCOTT-HENDERSON Oh, I know what you mean! I caught her in town yesterday. School hours, mind! I asked her, 'What are you doing here, Tulip?' And she tips her head onto one side as if she's Miss Innocence herself, and tells me: 'Oh, Mr Scott-Henderson. The police needed one extra person my age and size for an identity parade down at the station. They wouldn't say why they'd arrested the girl, but one of the officers did tell me he thought she might be Polish.

MR BARNES *laughing* Polish! Yes, that's it! The perfect Tulip touch!

MISS FERGUSON Careful. She's coming.

Walking up the verandah steps, **Tulip** *spots* **Natalie.**

TULIP Hey, Natalie! He says he's not bothering to light it till later.

MR BARNES Natalie? What are you doing, lurking there out of sight? Were you eavesdropping?

NATALIE No, no! I've only just come back myself.

MR BARNES Well, run along, both of you. This verandah's supposed to be a quiet place. For guests.

Tulip *and* **Natalie** *move out of earshot.*

NATALIE I know. Let's go and find your kitten.

TULIP Kitten?

NATALIE Well, cat, now, obviously.

TULIP I don't have a cat.

16

NATALIE Of course you do! You were carrying one the day Dad and I met you.

TULIP Oh! Oh, yes! So I was. *(clearly rattled)* Yes, well... Well, I had to give it away. *(gathering confidence)* You see, my dad's allergic.

NATALIE Oh, Tulip! What a shame for you. Why didn't you tell me?

TULIP I forgot. *(hastily)* Come on, Natalie. Let's go up to the attics to play dress-ups. *(moving back within earshot)* And I'll tell you all about the beautiful yellow silk dress I've won in this huge cornflakes competition.

*Everyone on the verandah pricks up their ears. This time, even **Natalie** is suspicious.*

NATALIE What cornflakes competition? There's nothing about a competition on any of **our** packets.

TULIP No. It was on a scratchcard inside.

NATALIE Strange **we** didn't get any scratchcards.

TULIP They only sent out a few. It's a special anniversary thing. That's why the prize was a yellow silk dress. It's the very same frock that the model wore in their very first advert.

*Behind **Tulip**'s back, **Miss Ferguson** purses her lips in disapproval. **Mrs Pettifer** sighs and shakes her head. **Mr Barnes** exchanges a meaningful glance with **Mr Scott-Henderson**, who taps the side of his nose knowingly with his finger. **Natalie**, clearly embarrassed, takes **Tulip**'s arm to hurry her away.*

MR BARNES See? The Tulip touch.

TULIP *overhearing* What?

NATALIE *hastily* Nothing. Nothing at all. He isn't talking about anything to do with you. Come on, Tulip. Quick. Let's go up to the attics.

Scene Four

In the attics. **Tulip** *is dressed as a ruffian.* **Natalie** *is dressed in old-fashioned finery, tottering about in high heels.* **Tulip** *hauls feather boas, muffs, a horsewhip and a military tunic out of a trunk.*

TULIP Look at this jacket. It's even got medals on it.

NATALIE I'm getting better in these heels.

TULIP We could be real actors. We'd be so famous. *(jamming a felt hat down hard on* **Natalie** *and flinging a headscarf round her own head)* Oh, Mrs Barraclough! Did you see the famous Tulip Pierce in that wonderful play last night on telly?

NATALIE *affecting a posh voice* Indeed I did, Mrs Henson. And did you notice that astonishingly talented young actress, Natalie Barnes?

TULIP Personally, I preferred Tulip.

NATALIE Well, I preferred Natalie.

TULIP No. Tulip.

NATALIE No. Natalie.

TULIP Tulip!

NATALIE Natalie!

Tulip whips off the headscarf and snatches up the horsewhip.

TULIP *in a grating, threatening man's voice* Don't mess with me! I'll peel you alive, like a banana! You even smile at me wrong today, and I will **crush** you!

NATALIE *unnerved* Tulip, stop it! You're making me nervous. Let's play something diff–

TULIP *unstoppable* Oh, yes. I'll make you sorry if you cross me today. I'll make those pretty eyes of yours look like slits in a grapefruit.

NATALIE *terrified* Tulip, stop it! Stop being – whoever you are. I hate it. Stop it!

Tulip *coming back to herself* Silly! It's only acting.

Natalie No, but it's horrible.

Tulip Honestly, Nats. You are **wet**. I was only being – someone I know really well – in a temper.

Natalie *shuddering* I hope I never meet them!

Tulip *turning back to the trunk* What else is in here? Oh, look! A ballgown. *(holding it against her)* Do you think this would fit me? Hey, Natalie! I've suddenly thought of something. The people who owned all these really old things must be dead. These are **dead** people's things we're wearing, aren't they?

Natalie *horrified* Ugh! (***Natalie** can't get out of her costume fast enough.* **Tulip** *stands clutching her armful even closer, smiling with glee.* **Tulip** *freezes.* **Natalie** *drops the last of her costume on the floor and steps forward to speak to the audience)* So, just like Mr Scott-Henderson, you might ask: *(imitating his incredulity)* 'What sort of magic does she **have** for you?' And I've spent hours wondering. And **still** I can't explain. Except to say that, somehow, everything I did without her seemed so drab and grey, and not worth doing. And games I played with her – even the creepy ones that scared me a little – seemed so alive, and real, and bright as fire. And fun without her seemed – like Christmas without presents – quite unthinkable.

Scene Five

In the hotel. **Natalie** *is pestering* **Mr Barnes** *and* **Mrs Barnes** *as they hang Christmas decorations and* **Julius** *arranges gift-wrapped boxes underneath the tree.*

Natalie You will let her come, won't you?

Mrs Barnes Natalie, I'm sure Tulip would far rather spend Christmas at home with her own family.

Julius She wouldn't. She **always** wants to be here, doesn't she, Natty? She says she wishes she didn't **ever** have to go home. She says she wishes she **lived** here.

MRS BARNES I'm sure she doesn't mean it, Julius.

JULIUS She does. Sometimes she just stands stroking bits of furniture, or the bannisters or something, and tells me and Natty we're the luckiest people in the whole world because we live here.

MRS BARNES But still… Christmas! It's a time for being with your own family.

JULIUS What about all the people who are coming to have Christmas here? They're not with their families.

MRS BARNES That's a bit different, Julius. They're paying to have a really nice time.

NATALIE Well, that's why Tulip wants to come. She says there's nothing special at her house.

MRS BARNES Oh, come now! They must have decorations.

NATALIE She says her dad says decorations are a waste of money. So her mum just shoves some old plastic nativity figures on the mantelpiece. And they're all manky anyway, says Tulip, from when she was a baby and chewed them.

MR BARNES She must have **presents**.

NATALIE Only things she needs. Last year she got a new school skirt. And a calculator because Miss Henson said she couldn't slow me up in maths any more by borrowing mine all the time.

MR BARNES Slowing you up? Good thing for you she got **that** present, then.

MRS BARNES And perhaps they all have something really special for Christmas lunch.

NATALIE They don't. They just have chicken. And Christmas pudding from a packet.

MRS BARNES But Natalie – Oh, look. Here's Tulip now.

Tulip rushes in and sweeps Natalie aside.

TULIP Did they say yes? Did they? Can I come here for Christmas? Can I?

NATALIE They said –

TULIP *to Mr Barnes* Oh, can I? Can I? Please! Pretty, pretty please!

MR BARNES But, Tulip. Won't your parents mind? Won't they want you at home with them?

TULIP *clearly lying* Oh, no. They don't mind. They say it's just a shame I don't have any brothers or sisters to share the day, and if I want to be with Natalie, they're happy for me.

Mr and Mrs Barnes exchange glances, and shrug.

MR BARNES In that case, my dear Tulip, I'm sure we'll be delighted to have you.

MISS FERGUSON *meanly* And you can wear that lovely yellow dress you told us you won in that cornflakes competition.

TULIP Oh, didn't I tell you? Mum spilled bleach on the sleeve by accident. So she's posted it off to a big firm in Chichester that does a lot of mending for the royal family, to see if they can patch it from the hem. And it's not back yet.

Tulip takes Natalie's arm and they rush off.

MR BARNES Does mending for the royal family! The Tulip touch. Poor little imp. What sort of squashing must she get at home, to think she has to make up all this stuff to impress us?

MRS BARNES You'd think she had more than enough brains to know better.

MRS PETTIFER Oh, she has brains all right. I'm told the only reason why she does so badly at school is because she's never there.

MISS FERGUSON Not that the teachers are sorry. Miss Henson told George the barman's sister that she's a real handful.

JULIUS No one in school likes Tulip – except for Natalie.

MRS BARNES How do you know that, darling?

JULIUS Natalie told me. They're always telling Tulip off. 'Please try and settle down. You're distracting everyone round you.' 'Now that's not what I told you to do, is it?' 'Tulip, I warn you, I have had enough!' 'If you two don't stop lolling against one another, I shall be forced to separate you.'

MRS BARNES Which 'you two' is this, Julius?

JULIUS Tulip and Natalie. They get in trouble all the time. And especially in Maths, because of what Natalie said, about sharing the calculator.

MR BARNES But Natty just told us Tulip was given a calculator.

JULIUS She was. But Mr Pierce hurled it against the wall when he was drunk. They've been back sharing again for ages.

MR BARNES Oh, this is too much! *(softly to Mrs Barnes)* I'm going to ask Miss Henson to separate the two of them.

JULIUS *overhearing* Miss Henson's tried that. But Natalie says everyone else kept moaning, 'Oh, don't make me sit by Tulip. She just mucks about.'

MRS BARNES Well, I certainly don't see why Natalie has to take the brunt of it.

JULIUS Natalie doesn't mind. She likes being with Tulip and Tulip likes being with her. They're famous for it. Miss Henson keeps telling Tulip, 'Natalie's not a puppet on a string' and she keeps telling Natalie, 'You're not Tulip's dummy, you know. You're supposed to have a mind of your own.'

MRS BARNES *anxiously* Puppet on a string?

MR BARNES *shocked* Dummy?

Tulip and Natalie cross in front of everyone, absorbed in some game. Tulip is walking backwards, manipulating a string puppet cross frame. Natalie staggers behind, walking as if she is a puppet being operated by Tulip's strings. Seeing nothing sinister, Julius just grins, but Mr Barnes and Mrs Barnes watch, frozen with horror.

Scene Six

In the hotel. Christmas Eve morning. Everyone is dressed up. **Tulip** *comes in, dressed as cheaply and drably as usual, and looking horribly out of place.*

Mr Barnes Morning, Tulip, my flower! Happy Christmas!

Tulip Am I in time for breakfast? Are there sausages?

Mr Barnes Breakfast? Haven't your parents even – ? Breakfast! Of course. But I do have to warn you that no one gets late breakfast in this hotel, even on Christmas Eve, without agreeing on the price first with the Manager.

Tulip *worried* What is it?

Mr Barnes Let's see... Holiday season... Special menu... Out of hours... So I'm afraid it's going to be – a hug and three kisses!

Tulip hugs him. **Mr Barnes** *swings her round.* **Mrs Barnes** *comes out of the office, holding a velvet frock.*

Mrs Barnes Ah, Tulip. I'm not sure quite how to put this, dear. You see this lovely dress? Well, it belongs to Mrs Stoddart's Cecily. But she's decided to wear her green one, and Mrs Stoddart and I thought this would fit you. It's just for today, mind. You mustn't run off with it.

Natalie *hissing* Mum, don't **say** that! You'll hurt Tulip's feelings!

Tulip does look offended.

Mr Barnes *hastily making a joke of it* And, Emma, I hope you've told Mrs Stoddart that she mustn't run off with Tulip, either. *(turning to* **Tulip***)* We want you here all day, don't we?

Tulip *ecstatic* All day! All day! Mr Barnes, when it gets dark, can I switch on the blinking lights?

Mr Barnes Yes, Tulip. You can switch on the blinking lights.

Tulip Oh, thank you! Thank you!

Natalie Come on. Let's put the dress on. See how you look. *(Tulip and Natalie rush behind a floor length curtain which bulges in places as Tulip changes. Out come Tulip's own clothes. Discreetly, Mrs Barnes removes them, wrinkling her nose a little, while the guests take drinks and nibbles off silver trays, mingle and chat. Natalie steps out and blows an imaginary fanfare)* Ta-raaa!

Shyly, Tulip steps out.

Mrs Pettifer Tulip! You look delightful!

Miss Ferguson Good heavens! What a transformation!

Guest 1 Such a pretty girl!

Guest 2 What an enchanting frock!

Mr Scott-Henderson Blimey! Is this our Tulip?

Guest 3 Tulip? What a lovely name! Tulip!

Julius You look terrific, Tule!

Mrs Stoddart There! Perfect fit.

Cecily I must be taller. The dress doesn't cover **my** shoes. Mind you, it doesn't **need** to…

Mrs Stoddart Hush, dear. If you can't say something pleasant…

The guests turn back to their conversations. Tulip stands in front of the mirror, enchanted with herself, stroking invisible puckers out of the velvet, practising dance swirls and curtseys, tipping her head to the side and smiling. We have a sense of hours passing. The light changes. Perhaps a grandfather clock face spins. The guests mingle and chat and lift drinks off trays. As it darkens, everyone gathers to watch Tulip press down a special switch. They applaud. Outside on the verandah, pink and orange and red lights blink, reminiscent of flickering fire. We hear a gong.

Mr Scott-Henderson Was that the dinner gong? I can hardly believe it.

Miss Ferguson I thought at lunch time that I'd never eat again. But, strangely enough, I feel quite peckish.

Mr Barnes lifts a canapé off a passing waiter's tray

MR BARNES Here, Tulip. Unbutton your beak!

NATALIE Dad, at dinner, will there be pies with battlements?

MR BARNES Natalie, when did we ever **not** have pies with battlements on Christmas Eve?

TULIP And will there be some of those great long pink fishes on a dish?

MR BARNES Salmon, Tulip. Yes, there'll be salmon. But by the time we're finished, it'll be really late. Are you sure you won't get in hot water?

TULIP *clearly lying* They know I'm probably going to stay the night. They said I could.

MR BARNES *disbelieving and anxious* Well, if you're **sure**...

*Tulip prances away happily. **Mr Barnes** and **Mr Scott-Henderson** watch her go.*

MR SCOTT-HENDERSON I reckon that poor scrap will end up paying a higher price than anyone else here for her Christmas dinner.

MRS PETTIFER *clapping her hands* Carols! Time to sing carols, everyone!

TULIP I'm off to brush my hair before the carols!

Tulip rushes out of the room.

MR BARNES And I expect she'll face a very different sort of music in the morning.

*The desk phone rings. **Mrs Barnes** goes to lift the receiver.*

MRS BARNES Palace Hotel. How may I help you? .. Sorry? ... **What?** *(replaces receiver, shocked)* Oh, my heavens!.

MR BARNES *hurrying over* What? What is it?

Mrs Barnes It was a message for Tulip. From her father.

Mr Barnes What? What was it? What did the man say?

Mrs Barnes He said – he said – oh, I can hardly bear it! He said, if the girl wasn't home in five minutes, he'd snatch her bald-headed.

Mr Barnes 'Snatch her **bald-headed**'? *(Mrs Barnes nods. The nearest guests, overhearing, fall silent, horrified. The chatter dies away outwards, till everyone is standing, silent and uneasy. Then **Mr Barnes** says to the nearest waiter)* Jamie! Drop that tray! Quickly! Go and fetch one of the cars round to the front. Leave the engine running. Quickly!

Jamie hands the tray to the nearest astonished guest, and runs out.

Mrs Barnes Her clothes! Her own clothes!

*Mrs Barnes rushes to fetch **Tulip**'s clothes.*

Mr Barnes She can change in the car. *(shouting)* Tulip! Tulip, where are you? Quick! Tulip! Quick!

ACT TWO

It's the following October. The scenes in this act can be played separately, or run seamlessly into one another. The action takes place between the school gates and the centre of town.

Scene One

*Natalie is hanging around the gates at the end of school. Pupils drift past, waving goodbye, running for buses, etc… A **girl** in one group stops.*

GLENYS Natalie, if you're not doing anything, why don't you come with us?

NATALIE Sorry. Waiting for Tulip.

MEGAN Tulip? Did she even come today?

ANDREW Bit of a rarity if she did.

GLENYS *to her friends* She bunked off Monday. But she was here yesterday. We couldn't have the ropes out in gym because she kept mucking about.

ANDREW She was so rude to Mrs Heller. All Helly asked her to do was get on with her work, and she swept everything off her desk onto the floor in a temper.

GLENYS *to Natalie* I bet you're glad your parents made the teachers separate you two in class. Tulip's **always** in trouble now.

JOSH I heard Mr Stanhope telling Mr Leroy how he can't stand her. 'All bold and sassy if you speak to her. But the minute she wants something from you, she turns into Little Miss Cute-and-Mincing'.

MEGAN You can't be Miss All-That-Cute-and-Mincing with raggedy hair you cut yourself with blunt nail scissors.

JOSH And fingernails bitten till they bleed.

GLENYS Ssh! She's Natalie's **friend**.

JOSH Can't be much of one. After all, she's hardly ever here. And when she is, she spends her whole time on report outside Mrs Golightly's office. *(to Natalie)* I don't know why you don't give up on her.

MEGAN Yes, forget Tulip. Come with us.

GLENYS Why don't you? We're off down town. Going to look for some poncy hair stuff for Andrew-the-boy-haystack.

ANDREW You said you **liked** my hair like this!

MEGAN *to Natalie* Coming?

NATALIE She said to meet here, so I ought to stay a little longer. Just in case she shows up...

MEGAN *shrugging* Your funeral.

They saunter off, chatting merrily. **Natalie** *looks after them wistfully.*

NATALIE Well, maybe, since she hasn't come...

MEGAN Yes. Come on, Natty!

NATALIE *lifting her schoolbag* Yes! I think I will.

ANDREW Uh-uh. Here's Tulip now. Sloping round the bike shed.

GLENYS Well, I'm not hanging about. She's got so **mean.** Do you know what she said to Marigold Henderson when she failed that maths test? She said...

Glenys and Megan go off, arm in arm, chatting.

ANDREW Coming, Natalie?

NATALIE Maybe tomorrow.

ANDREW If Tulip lets you.

JOSH *laughing* Yes. If Tulip lets her.

Andrew and Josh go off, laughing.

Scene Two

Tulip arrives, smiling and holding a small box.

TULIP Did you bring the wrapping paper?

NATALIE No.

TULIP Stupid! *(then she peers closely at Natalie)* Oh. You're lying, aren't you? I can tell, you know. And you have brought it, haven't you?

Tulip snatches Natalie's bag and roots in it.

NATALIE No, honestly. I couldn't find any! I–

Tulip holds up a sheet of fancy gift wrap paper.

TULIP Oh, no?

NATALIE Tulip, why don't we just forget it. It's a horrible idea.

TULIP *wrapping the box* No. It'll be a laugh. Wait till you see his face when he opens it.

NATALIE I really don't think we should... Look, the more I thought about it, the more...

TULIP You? Bird-brain? Think? Do me a favour!

NATALIE There's no need to be horrible, Tulip.

TULIP Sssh! He's coming. Now don't you dare go spoiling this, Natalie. *(Jamie comes out of school. Tulip prances out to stop him)* Hi, Jamie! Got a present for you.

JAMIE A present? Why?

TULIP *acting sweet and flirty* For your birthday.

JAMIE *suspicious* Bit late, isn't it?

TULIP *giggling* Well, I didn't realise till Marcie gave you those sweets. But I meant to anyway. I'd saved this up especially for you.

Miss Golightly appears, unnoticed, and stands watching.

JAMIE What is it?

TULIP A surprise.

Jamie takes the box.

NATALIE Tulip, don't –

TULIP *nastily to Natalie* Shut up! *(sweetly to Jamie)* Go on. Open it. It won't bite you.

Jamie opens the box.

JAMIE *disgusted* It's dog mess. It's real dog mess!

TULIP Happy birthday! *(Tulip stamps on Natalie's foot)* Go on, Natty. Say it!

NATALIE *muttering unwillingly* Happy birthday.

JAMIE You are disgusting! Both of you!

Jamie rushes off, clearly upset.

MRS GOLIGHTLY Tulip Pierce! Natalie Barnes! Come here at **once**!

Tulip stares, then takes to her heels.

TULIP Quick, Natalie! Run!

MRS GOLIGHTLY *warningly* Natalie! *(Natalie falters and comes back)* Is this the sort of little game you're playing now? You and your 'friend'? I am disgusted! Shocked! *(calmer now)* Think, Natalie! Think what you're doing! She's a very clever girl, Tulip. With a huge number of very real problems. But that's no reason **you** should be sucked in. Upsetting people. Wasting time. Disturbing lessons. And **worse.** *(Natalie hangs her head)* Have you ever thought why it is your parents got so worried about the two of you?

Natalie *resentfully* Not **that** worried.

Mrs Golightly *sharply* What do you mean?

Natalie Nothing.

Mrs Golightly *more gently* No, really. Tell me.

Natalie Well, all my Mum ever thinks about is the hotel. Oh, and Julius, of course! And Dad doesn't mind Tulip. He lets her come to The Palace whenever she wants.

Mrs Golightly Really? Whenever she wants?

Natalie Yes. She comes all the time.

Mrs Golightly Not the impression he gave me. And I'm sure he'd be happier if you invited some other, less – troubled – friends.

Natalie Tulip's no trouble at the hotel. No trouble at all. She loves The Palace. She says it's the only place she's ever really felt safe and happy.

Mrs Golightly Then I expect he feels sorry for her. I think we all do. And fair enough. But let me give you some good advice, Natalie. I've seen a good deal more of life than you have. And I can warn you. You'll come to no good at all as Tulip's hold-your-coat merchant. No good at all.

Voice off *calling* Mrs Golightly! Telephone!

Mrs Golightly hurries away.

Scene Three

Tulip sidles back.

Tulip Want to play 'Road of Bones' all the way home? No. Quick! Here comes Mrs Bodell. Let's play 'Stinking Mackerel'.

*Tulip pulls **Natalie** to her side. Together they mince towards **Mrs Bodell**, wrinkling their noses and sniffing as if at some noxious smell.*

Mrs Bodell *offended* I'm catching the bus into Urlinghame now. But as soon as I get back, I shall phone your head teacher. Don't think I don't know your parents, Natalie Barnes! **And** how ashamed they'll be to hear of your behaviour.

Mrs Bodell hurries off. Tulip and Natalie both snigger.

Tulip Brilliant! Well, what now? Home? Or 'Havoc!'?

Natalie Oh, well. I'll be in trouble anyway if she rings. We may as well play 'Havoc'.

Tulip Goody! What's it to be? A sweetie swipe?

Natalie No, Tulip! He watches us. He knows you're doing it. He can see in his little mirror.

Tulip Chicken! Lily-liver! I'll go by myself and see what I can get.

Tulip runs off. Natalie stares helplessly after her.

Scene Four

Mr Scott-Henderson strolls along and notices Natalie.

Mr Scott-Henderson Is that you, Natalie? Guess who I met at the bus stop. That Mrs Bodell woman. And aren't you in trouble with her! Something, of all things, about pretending she smells?

Natalie *sourly* How come it's Tulip who invents the games, and me who gets in trouble?

Mr Scott-Henderson Haven't you noticed yet, Natalie, that games with Tulip have always had a horrible habit of starting well for two, and ending up nastily for one. Remember that one she used to play with Julius called 'Putting On the Bag'?

Natalie Mum stopped that.

Mr Scott-Henderson And 'Babe In the Wood'? I remember hearing your mother tell Tulip if she ever upset Julius like that again, she'd be in big trouble.

Natalie In trouble… *(remembering)* Mr Scott-Henderson, what's a 'hold-your-coat merchant'?

Mr Scott-Henderson A hold-your-coat merchant? That's someone who likes to stand on the sidelines and watch someone **else** get in trouble. You know the type. *(imitating)* 'Go on! You fight him! He deserves it! I'll stand here safely and I'll hold your coat.' Whoops! There's my lift! Bye!

Mr Scott-Henderson hurries off. Natalie stands thinking.

Scene Five

Tulip comes back dragging an unwilling Marcie.

Tulip I bumped into Marcie. She was in the shop with me.

Marcie *irritated* Got thrown out of the shop **because** of you is more like it. *(to Natalie)* He thought she was on the take, so he threw everyone under ninety out. *(to Tulip)* He really doesn't trust you, you can tell.

Tulip He likes me.

Natalie Oh, Tulip! that's not true. I told you, he **hates** it when we go in there. He watches you all the time.

Tulip No, he doesn't. He offered me a real job yesterday.

Marcie Don't be so silly. Nobody offers a real job to anyone our age.

Tulip He did. He said it was 'unofficial'. He said – he said I reminded him of his little sister, who choked to death on pencil sharpenings.

Marcie *incredulous* On **pencil sharpenings**?

Natalie *softly* The Tulip Touch!

Tulip What?

Natalie Nothing.

MARCIE I don't believe you, Tulip. It's just another of your stupid lies. And I'm off home now.

TULIP No, wait. I've got something to show you.

MARCIE No, thanks.

TULIP Really! It's brilliant. I got it yesterday. It's in my bag.

Tulip roots in her bag and brings out a gold necklace.

MARCIE Where did you get that? Did you **steal** it?

TULIP It's mine.

NATALIE Is it real gold?

TULIP Of course.

MARCIE *taking it* It **is** real gold. It's got that funny mark. It can't be yours.

TULIP It is.

MARCIE *looking Tulip up and down* I don't think so. It must be worth an awful lot.

TULIP *hotly* Why shouldn't it be mine?

MARCIE *handing the necklace to Natalie* Same reason the police got called when Josh lost his watch. And Mr Patrick lost his wallet. I'm off now. I don't spend time with thieves. Are you coming, Natalie?

NATALIE *whispering* Tulip, you really ought to take this back to wherever you –

MARCIE I said, are you coming? Or are you staying here with Little Miss Thief.

TULIP You'll be sorry you called me that, Marcie!

Tulip chases off threateningly after Marcie. Natalie stands holding the necklace as if it's red hot, biting her lip in indecision.

Scene Six

Tulip comes back, grinning. She pockets the necklace.

TULIP So what now? Bottle smash? Or dustbin fire?

NATALIE Oh, no! Not a dustbin fire, Tulip.

TULIP They're brilliant. All those colours! And it's just rubbish anyhow. You're doing people a favour really. But anyway they're better when it's dark and that'll be ages.

NATALIE I should be getting home now. I told Mum –

TULIP *not even listening* Oh, excellent! Road kill!

Tulip pulls a plastic bag from her pocket and scoops up the dead pigeon she's just spotted.

NATALIE I can't **believe** you keep those in your pocket just in case you find something dead.

TULIP Always useful. Now where shall we put it? Oh, look! A rabbit! He'll like some quiet company.

Tulip scrambles over a fence into a garden.

NATALIE Tulip, can't you even wait to check no one's looking!

TULIP Baby! Scaredy cat! (*Natalie follows. Holding the bag, **Tulip** lifts the rabbit out of his hutch)* Well, hello, Thumper. Let's make some room here for your little dead friend.

91

NATALIE Tulip, you're not holding him right! Be gentle! *(uneasy)* Look, why don't you let me take him?

TULIP How do you know he's a he? He might be a she.

NATALIE It doesn't matter. Just let me hold him.

TULIP Only if you've guessed right. No! She's a she. So she's **mine**.

NATALIE She's not **yours**, Tulip.

TULIP She is now. *(Tulip holds the rabbit close and begins to croon)* Who's a clever bunny? Who's going to be a good girl? Who's Tulip's special one? *(Gradually, Tulip's voice gets gruffer and deeper, until they are the same threatening 'ruffian' tones with which, holding the horsewhip, she frightened Natalie in the attics. It's clearly someone else's voice, and intensely menacing. Natalie's unease deepens to horror)* She's not going to make a fuss, is she? Oh, no. She isn't going to do that. Because she enjoys it really, doesn't she? And, if she starts struggling, she'll get **hurt.**

NATALIE Tulip! Stop saying those horrid things! Put the poor thing down! *(As if a spell has been broken, Tulip comes back to herself. She dumps the rabbit back in the hutch)* Quick! Someone's watching. Hurry up!

TULIP *scornfully* There's no one watching. *(Natalie scrambles back over the fence. Tulip saunters back, insolently swiping off flowerheads)* You'll have to go back for the pigeon.

NATALIE Me? Why me? It's your – dead thing. You're the one who left it there. You go.

TULIP No. You go.

Sighing, Natalie creeps back for the bag while Tulip smiles.

NATALIE I don't see why it has to be me.

TULIP *contemptuously* Oh, don't you?

NATALIE *stung* No, I don't.

TULIP You just don't get it, do you, Natalie. You're the Princess who lives in The Palace, who always has to be neat and tidy and good and polite, and hold her fork properly and never make trouble. So it's easy enough for me to see why you need someone to lead your secret life for you. Someone to be bad while you have to stay perfect. I know why **you** chose **me**. But surely, surely, even someone as stupid as you has managed to work out why I chose you. Now, give me the bag. *(Natalie hands it over. Tulip struggles to wrap it up again)* And, here! Hold my coat!

Tulip thrusts her jacket into Natalie's hand. Natalie looks down at it and stares.

Mrs Golightly *as a voiceover* I warn you, Natalie, you'll come to no good as Tulip's hold-your-coat merchant. No good at all.

Mr Scott-Henderson *as a voiceover* A hold-your-coat merchant? Why, that's someone who likes to stand on the sidelines and watch someone **else** get in trouble.

As if scorched, **Natalie** *thrusts the jacket away on a nearby bench.*

Scene Seven

Tulip I know. We'll play 'Little Visits'.

Natalie Little visits?

Tulip Yes. Watch. I tried it out while I was bunking off today. You give yourself points for getting inside people's houses. *(Tulip strides up to the nearest house.* **Natalie** *watches.* **Tulip** *speaks animatedly to the woman on the doorstep, who, after a moment's doubt, lets her in.* **Natalie** *watches, astonished. After a few moments,* **Tulip** *rushes out)* See? Easy!

Natalie What did you **say** to her?

Tulip I told her I was looking for Torrington Avenue, and did she have a map?

Natalie She let you in for that!

Tulip Why shouldn't she? Sometimes I told people I needed a pencil and paper to write down the car number of someone who went over a red light. Sometimes I just asked if I could phone my mother, and then say it's engaged. For it to count, you have to get both feet over the doorstep. And, once you're in, you have to change something.

Natalie What sort of thing?

Tulip Well, you could swivel a photo round to face the wall.

Natalie Or swap round the ornaments?

Tulip Anything. This morning, I took someone's scissors off the table and stabbed them, points down, in a plant pot.

NATALIE *intrigued despite herself* And does everyone let you in?

TULIP Not everyone. Some people are dead suspicious. That's what's so good about the game. You can't be sure.

NATALIE Can I try?

TULIP Pick a house. I'll watch.

NATALIE This one. *(Natalie creeps up a path and knocks. A **man** opens the door. Natalie speaks. The **man** shakes his head and makes to close the door. Natalie speaks more animatedly. He changes his mind and lets her in. Tulip hugs herself with glee. A moment or two later, **Natalie** comes flying out, exhilarated)* It was brilliant! Brilliant! I was so clever! Did you see me?

TULIP Of course I saw. What did you say?

NATALIE I asked him for a glass of water.

TULIP He didn't want to give it you at first.

NATALIE No. But then I told him – *(excited)* I told him, *(re-enacting)* I never used to knock on people's doors to ask for water. But since the problem with my throat, with swallowing, well it's been difficult. Because last time I was in hospital, the doctors thought they'd got rid of the lump for ever. Because it's very unusual, in someone my age. So everyone was very disappointed when it came back. *(grinning)* And by then, I was in.

TULIP See? It's a great game! 'Little Visits'!

NATALIE 'Little Visits'!

They go off arm in arm, laughing.

Scene Eight

TULIP Well, what shall we do now?

NATALIE You choose.

TULIP *scooping up mud* We could flick mud pellets. But I'm not wasting them on men this time. Only on women wearing really light colours.

NATALIE You're not to do it at this lady coming now. The poor thing can only just walk!

*A tired **old man** approaches, carrying heavy bags.*

TULIP It's not a lady, stupid. It's a man. *(she drops the mud pellet, steps forward and says in her false, sweet voice)* I'm sorry, but there's no point coming this way. The alley's blocked at the other end.

OLD MAN But this is my shortcut. I can't manage to walk all the way round.

TULIP You'll have to, I'm afraid. You see, there's been the most terrible murder and the police have blocked it off.

NATALIE Tulip! You mustn't tell him that. He's far too ol–

TULIP Ssssh!

OLD MAN *distressed* Oh, dear. Oh, dear.

*The **old man**, exhausted, turns back.*

NATALIE Tulip, that is so **mean.**

TULIP You're so **soft**, Natalie. So what are we doing now?

NATALIE I'm going home.

TULIP You're mad at me, aren't you? Is little Goody-Two-Shoes cross with her big bad nasty friend?

NATALIE *irritated* No.

TULIP Oh yes, you are. Don't forget you can't keep secrets from me. I can read minds. And especially yours. Easy!

NATALIE Stop saying that!

TULIP What?

NATALIE That you can read my mind. I hate it.

TULIP Well, I can. I've got the knack of it.

Natalie Oh, yes! Another little Tulip touch?

Tulip *suspicious* What do you mean?

Natalie It doesn't matter. And anyway, I'm going now. I've just remembered I promised Mum I'd be home early to help her do the menus for next week.

Tulip You're lying, Natalie. You're making it up to try and get away. Nobody notices when you get home. You know that. Your mum and dad are always too busy sucking up to the guests. *(mincing)* 'Oh, let me fetch you another gin and tonic, Mrs Snobby-Wobby.' 'Oh, Mr Fancy Bow-tie! Did I forget to order your paper?' 'Was the room to your satisfaction, Lady Muck-Pot?'

Natalie Shut up!

Forgetting her bag, **Natalie** *strides away.* **Tulip** *shouts after her.*

Tulip Nobody notices **you.** And even if the guests all dropped down dead, your mother would still only notice her precious Julius. *(imitating)* 'Oh, Julius, dear! Let me put a plaster on that teensy-weensy graze on your knee. I know your sister's just been run over, but **you're** the important one.'

Natalie has her hands over her ears. **Tulip** *kicks* **Natalie***'s bag into the side of the road, and storms off the other way.* **Natalie** *creeps back, picks up her muddy schoolbag, sinks down, puts her head in her hand and weeps.*

Scene Nine

Tulip *rushes back, wildly excited.*

Tulip I **thought** you wouldn't have got far! Listen! I just heard the most amazing news!

Natalie I don't want to know. In fact, you've been so horrid I don't even want to be your fr–

Tulip Just listen! Janet Brackenbury's sister has drowned.

NATALIE What, Muriel? Oh, how awful! Poor Janet! Oh!

TULIP *eyes shining* Just think! We know someone whose sister is **dead. Drowned.**

NATALIE Don't keep **saying** that!

TULIP We could sell our stories to the paper. We could be photographed with our arms around Janet.

NATALIE Don't be so silly. Janet doesn't even like us.

TULIP I bet she's so **upset.** She won't be able to stop thinking about it. *(with relish)* Thrashing about in the water! Her last air bubbles shooting up – *(**Natalie** stares in horror and growing realisation as, almost hysterically, **Tulip** rants on)* All that scrabbling to try and find something to grab hold of! I expect you swallow so much that, when they find you, you're all swollen up. Not like with kittens. I bet Janet'll wake practically every night now, imagining it over and over, and not being able to –

*Natalie lays a hand on **Tulip**'s arm, to stop her.*

NATALIE You drowned that kitten, didn't you?

TULIP *spell broken* What kitten?

NATALIE *calmly* The one you were cuddling the day we met. I always thought it was your dad who got rid of all the kittens. But it was you.

TULIP No, it wasn't.

*Natalie settles on a low wall and pats it. Obediently, **Tulip** sits beside her.*

NATALIE *so gently* Tulip, I know in your eyes it's the **world** that's wrong. If things had only been **fairer,** you wouldn't need to lie, or steal, or be spiteful. If the **world** was only right, you'd be a good and nice person, the girl you are inside, the girl you were before it all went wrong and you got spoiled all along with it.

TULIP *still subdued* What are you talking about?

Natalie Your lies, and meanness and stuff. That's why you don't see how it looks to other people. Because you know it shouldn't really be the way it is, but the **other** way. The way you like to tell it. But you did drown those kittens, didn't you?

Tulip I **had** to. Who else was going to do it? Not Mum. She's so scared of Dad, she just does what she's told and keeps her head down. She's too busy worrying about her next pasting to care about any old kittens. And I can't let Dad do it. I just can't. All he does is shove them in a crock of water and shove down the lid. And you can hear them scrabbling and pushing at the top. And it takes forever. It takes hours and hours.

Natalie *gently* Not hours, Tulip. I bet it seemed like it. But kittens wouldn't be strong enough. Honestly. Not hours.

Tulip Long enough. So ever since then, I've always done it myself. Because it's quicker. And once they're under, I never let them up again. *(fiercely)* No. Not ever!

*Natalie puts her arm around **Tulip**'s shoulders. **Tulip** weeps quietly. Natalie pulls out a tissue and mops **Tulip**'s face. Then she slides off the wall and holds out a hand to her.*

Natalie Come along, Tulip. Time to go home.

Scene Ten

*By the school gates. **Tulip** marches up, dressed in black. A **teacher** stops her. Passing **pupils** linger to watch.*

Teacher Tulip, the correct colour for sweaters in this school is blue.

Tulip *smugly* But I'm wearing black for Muriel.

Teacher Muriel?

Tulip Muriel Brackenbury. *(with relish)* Who **drowned**.

Teacher Good heavens! You can have barely known the girl!

Tulip *insolently* So?

Tulip *makes to swagger past. The **teacher** steps in front.*

TEACHER Tulip Pierce! This is self-indulgence stretched into morbidity. And hardly likely to comfort poor Janet! Take off that pullover at once.

TULIP It's none of your business.

TEACHER It most certainly is. And I warn you, you're not coming into school dressed like that.

TULIP Then I'm not coming in at all!

Tulip runs off.

TEACHER Where are you running off to? What are you doing?

TULIP *menacingly* You'll see! Oh, just you wait! You'll see!

Scene Eleven

Beside a semi-derelict chicken shed. (The fire in this scene will owe everything to clever lighting, projection and sound.) **Tulip** *drags* **Natalie** *closer.*

NATALIE I keep telling you! I can't hang around today. My mum and dad are waiting.

TULIP You wish! And you're my **friend**. I don't want you to miss this. I've been working on it all day. It's going to be brilliant!

NATALIE What's that smell?

TULIP Petrol! It's taken me all day to get enough.

NATALIE Enough? Are all those cans full of petrol?

TULIP They were. They're not now. And now you're going to see something that makes even our very best dustbin fires look like a damp squib.

Tulip lights a match.

NATALIE No, Tulip! No!

Tulip sets fire to a petrol trail.

TULIP Watch, Natalie!

The fire flares up, first flickering on their faces like the Christmas decorations on the verandah, then more brightly.

NATALIE Tulip, you're mad! Suppose there's someone in there! Some tramp, asleep! Or drunk!

TULIP Stop fussing, Natalie! Enjoy it! Look at it. It's brilliant. It's our best yet, by far!

NATALIE Yes, but... *(losing her thread, she stares, fascinated)* Oh, Tulip! Look at it! Fizzing!

TULIP Crackling!

NATALIE I can see shooting stars!

TULIP I can see fireballs!

NATALIE Scorching the sky!

TULIP Magic gone crazy!

NATALIE *wistfully* Oh, Tulip! It's so beautiful. So very, very beautiful...

TULIP *almost with spite* See? Not so goody-goody after all, are you? A little bit tougher, and you could be just like me!

NATALIE *not even listening* It's like some great orange dragon leaping higher and higher. It's – it's – oh, Tulip! It's so wonderful! Thank you! Thank you!

We hear sirens coming closer.

TULIP Natalie! Quick! Or we'll get caught! The police always suspect anyone standing and watching!

NATALIE *shaking her off* No, no. I'm staying. I'm watching till the end.

TULIP Natalie, you can't!

NATALIE *still struggling* Let me go, Tulip. Leave me be!

TULIP Natalie! *(Tulip drags the spell-bound **Natalie** out of sight. We hear the sound of engines and the shouts of fire officers as, gradually, **Natalie** comes to her senses. **Tulip** shakes **Natalie**)* Natalie! Natalie!

*Natalie stares at **Tulip**, appalled.*

NATALIE Tulip, you're mad! You're mad and dangerous! Julius used to **play** in that shed, when he was younger. He didn't come out, even if you called. He'd just tuck himself in tighter, out of sight, under the shelves.

TULIP Sssh! Better see if it's safe to go.

Tulip moves away to check what's happening.

NATALIE And kids don't **think**, if they smell petrol. Even lots of it. They don't think some crazy person's going to come along and... *(**Natalie** breaks off and turns to stare at **Tulip**. When she speaks again, it is to herself, in a whisper)* Some crazy person... *(inching away)* as dangerous as one of their own blazing fires. But don't say anything, Natty. No, no. Sssh! Poke a fire, and it flares even more fiercely. Everyone knows that. No. The only safe thing is to stay away! Stay away!

Tulip returns.

TULIP All clear. We'll slide round this way, and get back through the woods. We'll go to The Palace –

NATALIE We've got workmen. Dad says he doesn't want extra visitors.

TULIP We'll muck about where he won't see us, then.

NATALIE No! He'll be everywhere. There's a special wedding party.

TULIP That's never stopped us before. We'll stay out of sight! We can go on the roof. Play 'Watch the Skies'. Or 'All the Grey People'!

NATALIE No, Tulip.

Tulip stares. There is an uneasy silence.

TULIP *recovering* Oh, you'll change your mind on the way back. You'll see. *(as Tulip turns to pick up her coat, Natalie vanishes behind the hedge)* Then we can – Natalie? Natalie, where are you? *(searching)* Natalie! This isn't funny. Come out! Come on! I've just thought up a brilliant new game! 'In A Dark Wood'. Oh, come on out, Nat! Don't be stupid! *(Tulip wanders off, still calling)* Natalie! Natalie!

Breathing more easily, Natalie comes out, and goes off the other way.

ACT THREE

Scene One

It's a month later, back in The Palace. **Natalie** *strolls round, handing out newspapers. She looks different somehow – older, less tentative.* **Julius** *peeps round a curtain.*

JULIUS *whispering* Natalie! Hi, Natty! She's here **again**.

NATALIE *firmly* Tell her I'm busy.

JULIUS I **can't** just keep telling her you're busy.

NATALIE Why not?

JULIUS Well, she's supposed to be your **friend**. And she's got no one else. I just feel sorry for her.

NATALIE Well, don't! It's only a trap. But you watch out, because *(wriggling her fingers at him threateningly)* when she's not busy snarling at people, and slashing bus seats, and stealing stuff, and getting into fights, and swearing at the teachers, she'll use that Tulip touch of hers to suck you in, and make you bury all your own feelings down so deep, you practically won't realise you have them. *(Tulip appears on the verandah in a stained sweater and a badly-hemmed skirt)* And then, if you're not careful, she'll take over your – *(Julius signals frantically. Natalie glances behind her)* Tulip!

TULIP Natalie. *(nastily)* Still 'busy'?

Julius slips away.

NATALIE *gabbling nervously* I am, really. I've a load of homework. And then Mum wants a bit of help with the –

TULIP Natty, you can't fool **me**. Oh, you can turn into a good girl, and dress neatly, and make some nice new friends, and even start getting commendations for your schoolwork. And everyone else will be delighted. Since your parents are too busy even to **look** at you properly, they certainly won't notice how pale you've become. How much you've changed. **They** might not notice this 'new you' is just some pretend person you've tucked inside yourself, to say 'Good Morning' politely, and pass the beans, and hope you'll grow into. But **Tulip** knows...

NATALIE Leave me alone!

TULIP Aren't you missing me? Even a little? Missing our brilliant games? Don't you want to play 'Havoc'? Or 'Hogs in a Tunnel'? It's years since we played that. How about 'Road of Bones'? *(advancing)* Or would you rather have a dustbin fire? You really loved those fires, didn't you? You'd never admit it, but they brought some nice bright colours into your drab little 'good-girl' life.

NATALIE I'll find my own colours for my own life, thank you!

TULIP How? You're too stupid to think up your **own** games.

NATALIE Don't call me stupid, Tulip! Or I'll call **you** –

Natalie breaks off.

TULIP *taunting* What?

NATALIE *lightly* Nothing.

*But Natalie deliberately looks **Tulip**'s cheap, grubby clothing up and down, and wrinkles her nose.*

TULIP Oh, ho? so we **are** playing one of our old games, are we? 'Stinking Mackerel'! I'd practically forgotten that. Well, that makes it **my** turn to choose. And, believe me, Natalie. You might not reckon you and your precious family are playing. But I'll make sure I pick the very best game of all. **And** I'll make sure I win.

Tulip runs off. Mr Scott-Henderson walks in the way Tulip left. Julius comes in the way he left.

MR SCOTT-HENDERSON Was that our friend Tulip? We haven't seen her for a good few weeks.

NATALIE Well, she's been very busy. So have I. *(turning away)* Miss Ferguson! Here's your evening paper!

MR SCOTT-HENDERSON Well, never mind. Not long till Christmas. I take it she'll be coming, as usual.

NATALIE Well, **I'm** not inviting her.

MR SCOTT-HENDERSON Pity. I've always had a soft spot for your little friend.

NATALIE *sourly* She's not so little. *(overly sweetly)* But, if you're going to miss her **that** much, I could always tell you exactly where she lives, and you could invite her as **your** guest.

Mr Scott-Henderson hastily disappears behind his Evening News. Natalie walks off with the rest of the papers.

MISS FERGUSON Good heavens! What sauce! Almost **rude**.

MRS PETTIFER She's not the mouse she used to be, is she? That quiet little shadow of Tulip's is quite coming into her own!

MISS FERGUSON Downright pert, if you want my opinion.

Julius follows Natalie.

JULIUS Is that true? Are you really not inviting her? Not even for Christmas Eve?

NATALIE No, I'm not. After all, they can't have it both ways? Only last week, they were both saying how pleased they were I'm getting on so much better at school. Dad even told Mrs Golightly I used to waste my life floating round in a 'waiting-for-Tulip' cloud, and now I'm a different person.

JULIUS But, Christmas!

NATALIE Well, **you** invite her.

JULIUS *shivering* No, thanks. She frightens me. People in my class call her Crazy Tulip. And Harry's mother says she gives her the shivers. She says Tulip has a look about her, as if one day she'll start to scream and scream, and never stop.

Mrs Barnes comes over.

MRS BARNES Is this true, Natalie? What everyone's saying, that you're not inviting Tulip for Christmas?

NATALIE Why should I invite her for Christmas? I haven't invited her for weeks.

MRS BARNES I hadn't realised.

*The desk phone rings. **Mrs Barnes** rushes to pick it up.*

NATALIE *muttering bitterly* Well, you're always a bit busy, aren't you?

Mr Barnes comes over.

MR BARNES Natalie, what's all this I hear? Tulip has always **loved** Christmas at The Palace.

NATALIE Well, I love Christmas as well. And I don't feel like inviting her this year.

MR BARNES But she doesn't have much of a life, does she? So it would be nice. *(to a nearby guest)* She's such a scrap of a thing! And she has **such** a thin time of it at home. So we do try to give her at least one really special day.

NATALIE Look, Tulip's not **my** job. It's not **my** fault her dad's a bully and her mother's so weak she can't even stick up for her.

MR BARNES I thought she was your **friend**. Remember when my camera flash went off, and later, on that photo I hadn't even realised I took, we saw her sad, pale little face?

NATALIE *sighing* I know, I know. You said she looked **haunted.**

MR BARNES **Desolate** was more like it.

JULIUS Leave Natty alone! You say, 'Look after Tulip.' But Mrs Golightly told Natalie **not** to be her hold-your-coat merchant. You say, 'Be nice to Tulip.' But what you actually mean is, 'Don't get sucked in too far. Don't go round in a dream, waiting for her to come, with her exciting games and her brilliant ideas. Don't let her distract you in school, or stop you from doing your homework.' Well, that's like saying, 'Go play with the witch, but don't let her cast any spells on you.' And it's **not fair**!

*There is an astonished silence into which walk **two police officers***

OFFICER 1 *enquiring generally* Mr and Mrs Barnes?

MR SCOTT-HENDERSON *nodding* Over there.

OFFICER 1 Mrs Barnes –

The phone on the desk rings.

MRS BARNES Oh, Martin! You take that. I'll deal with this.

Mr Barnes beckons a member of staff over to take guests' orders for drinks as he picks up the telephone.

MRS BARNES *hurrying towards the officers* May I help you?

OFFICER 1 *ushering her away from the guests* The thing is, Mrs Barnes, we were rather hoping to have a word with your daughter Natalie.

Julius and Natalie exchange glances.

MRS BARNES *shocked* Natalie? But why?

OFFICER 2 If we might just have a word with her? In your presence, of course.

MRS BARNES *after a moment's doubt* Natalie.

Natalie approaches.

OFFICER 2 The thing is, Natalie, we've come about some little visits.

NATALIE 'Little Visits'? But we haven't played that for –

Natalie breaks off.

OFFICER 2 Sorry?

Natalie stares at her shoes.

MRS BARNES *mystified* Little visits? What little visits?

OFFICER 2 You see, Mrs Barnes, we're having a little problem with Tulip Pierce.

MRS BARNES Oh, Tulip! I might have known!

OFFICER 2 And we were wondering if Natalie here could help us understand.

MRS BARNES Understand what?

OFFICER 2 Why on earth Tulip might be doing what she's doing.

MRS BARNES And what on earth's that?

OFFICER 1 We've had a complaint. It seems Tulip Pierce has made three little visits to the family of that poor girl who drowned a while back. She keeps coming up to Mrs Brackenbury's door, and knocking, and asking her...

MRS BARNES *prompting* Asking her...?

OFFICER 1 Asking her if Muriel would like to come for a walk.

MRS BARNES I'm not sure I'm quite following...

OFFICER 1 Muriel **Brackenbury**. The girl who **drowned.**

MRS BARNES *appalled* Tulip is **visiting** them? And asking after their dead **daughter**?

OFFICER 2 Standing there on the doorstep.

OFFICER 1 Grinning all over her face.

MRS BARNES But that's disgusting! That's horrible! That is the worst, the sickest – *(to **Natalie**)* Do you **hear** this? I hope I never again hear of you spending time with Tulip Pierce! Do you understand what it is these officers are **saying**?

OFFICER 1 That's why we're here, Mrs Barnes. Because, when we asked around, we heard that Natalie may know Tulip well enough to help us understand exactly what it is we're dealing with here.

MRS BARNES You want to know if Tulip's mad, or bad?

OFFICER 1 That's not how we'd put it, of course. But if your daughter..: *(to **Natalie**)* Natalie, can you help us out? Can you tell us what might be going on here? Because, first time, the Brackenburys thought it must just be some horrible mistake.

MRS BARNES As indeed anyone would!

OFFICER 1 As they indeed would. With the result that they only rang us the second time. And I'm afraid we made exactly the same mistake. Just assumed someone had got the wrong end of the stick. Upsetting, of course, but perfectly innocent.

OFFICER 2 But then, for the third time, this evening...

NATALIE This **evening?**

MRS BARNES She's mad! There has to be something wrong with her! People's feelings aren't dice, to be played with. She has to be insane!

OFFICER 2 Natalie? Can you help us? Do you have any idea at all what all these little visits could be about? Could it be some sort of **dare?** Or **game?**

NATALIE *hastily* I don't know. We never did **anything** like that. Honestly. Nothing at all! But I don't see Tulip any more. I stopped seeing her ages ago. I've been so busy with my homework. And helping here, of course.

*Officer 1 looks long and hard at **Natalie**, who cracks and looks down.*

OFFICER 2 Well, any time. *(handing her a card)* Here's my number. Anything you think of that might help – anything at all – phone any time.

*Natalie nods. **Mrs Barnes** ushers the **officers** towards the door.*

MRS BARNES Honestly, I don't know what Natalie ever saw in Tulip Pierce.

OFFICER 1 Perhaps, Mrs Barnes, it's time to start wondering just what it was that Tulip saw in Natalie.

NATALIE What's going to happen to Tulip now?

OFFICER 1 Oh, we'll have a little chat with her. She won't go bothering the Brackenbury's again.

NATALIE *catching her arm* Promise me you won't tell her father! Promise me!

MRS BARNES They'll have to speak to Tulip's parents, Natalie.

NATALIE *almost hysterical* Oh, please! You mustn't! If you tell Mr Pierce, he'll kill her! I know he will!

MRS BARNES Nonsense, Natalie.

OFFICER 1 Don't you worry. We'll take it very gently. I think we all know about Mr Pierce's temper.

NATALIE No! You don't understand! If you tell him what she's been doing, he'll half-murder her. He'll just be glad to have the chance. He'll sound reasonable enough while you're there. But the minute you're gone – *(everyone in the room is now watching)* He's done it before. He enjoys it! He warns her! *(imitating Tulip's 'ruffian' voice)* 'Tulip, I'm going to thrash you like a red-headed stepchild! Oh, I'm going to whip you till your freckles **sing**!'

*Everyone stares, appalled. The **officers** are silent. Then they eye one another, put on their caps and hurry away.*

Scene Two

In the hotel, later.

MR SCOTT-HENDERSON It might have been a misunderstanding. That's always possible.

MISS FERGUSON Nonsense! It was wickedness! Pure wickedness!

MRS PETTIFER Ruth! The poor child is obviously deeply disturbed.

Mrs Barnes walks behind, carrying flowers.

MISS FERGUSON Oh, really! That Pierce girl is simply malevolent by nature. And part of the problem for children like her is that there are far too many people like you telling them *(imitating)* 'you **understand** how **hard** things are for them', and not enough like me who are prepared to say quite openly that their behaviour is downright **evil.**

MR SCOTT-HENDERSON *sarcastically* Oh, I see! Bad seeds, are they? Spawn of the devil?

MISS FERGUSON That's **right.** And when I was a girl, these things were made perfectly clear to us. We even had to learn a little poem. 'Satan is glad when I am bad.'

Mr Barnes pauses, walking past, to listen.

MR SCOTT-HENDERSON Oh, I remember that! *(stands to declaim)*
'Satan is glad
When I am bad
And hopes that I
With him shall lie
In fire and chains
And awful pains.'

MRS PETTIFER Scarcely a **poem.** More **doggerel,** I'd say.

Mr Barnes and Mrs Barnes meet at the desk.

MRS BARNES Miss Ferguson's quite right. Tulip is downright **evil.**

Julius, doing homework behind, lifts his head to listen.

MR BARNES I can't believe I'm hearing you right, Emma. You know those old frost-tops are light years from knowing the first thing about children. No one is born evil. No one. And especially not Tulip.

Julius signals Natalie to come and listen too.

Mrs Barnes *angrily arranging the flowers* I don't know how else you'd explain something so horrible.

*Natalie pretends to help **Julius** with his homework.*

Mr Barnes Oh, don't be silly. You know as well as I do that Tulip's had such a rotten start in life that it's hardly a surprise she's insensitive to other people's feelings.

Mrs Barnes This is a bit more than being insensitive!

Mr Barnes You know what I mean. To really know right from wrong, you need a certain emotional sympathy. And you only learn that from being treated properly yourself.

Mrs Barnes marches off to fetch another vase.

Mrs Barnes Tulip's not stupid. She knows the rules.

*Mr Barnes follows her. **Natalie** and **Julius** subtly alter position to keep listening.*

Mr Barnes Why should she think rules matter? Her father's are vindictive and wilful, and it must seem to her that, **whatever** she does, she gets punished. So why should she bother about rules?

Mrs Barnes Because she's bright enough to see that if enough people like her go round doing exactly what they want, **everyone's** miserable.

Mr Barnes If you've been brought up as if your feelings don't matter, you probably assume other people's don't matter much either.

Mrs Barnes Don't kid yourself. Tulip knows perfectly well how much other people's feelings matter. And that's exactly why she does these things. That's the amusement she gets from them. Why else would she do it?

Mr Barnes *shrugging* Well, you only have to pick up a paper to read about kids a lot younger doing worse.

56

MRS BARNES Children with violent tempers, I can understand. Even children with too few brains to see how dangerous a game is getting. But Tulip's visits to the Brackenbury's are out of another box. They're not just bad, They're **different**. And that's what evil is. Something **different**.

MR BARNES There's no such thing as evil. You know that. Look, Emma. Even professionals come across the odd child they just can't stand. The child they can't help thinking is deeply, deeply mean inside. And then what usually happens is that they meet the parents. And they begin to think, 'Poor little brute! No wonder the child's such a horror.'

MRS BARNES Then I've got a brilliant idea! Why don't you take Mr and Mrs Pierce round to meet Mrs Brackenbury. Then she can start feeling sorry for Tulip.

Mrs Barnes storms out with the vase. Mr Barnes follows.

JULIUS Phew! Not like them to have a barney **down**stairs!

Natalie spots the newspaper under his books.

NATALIE Is this this evening's? I thought you were supposed to be doing your **homework**.

Natalie and Julius don't notice Mr Barnes coming back.

Julius *embarrassed* Oh, I was just checking a few things.

NATALIE What? *(snatching the paper)* The fire in Urlinghame? Or that horrible, horrible stabbing in Bridleford? *(Julius is suddenly very busy with his work)* **What** were you checking, Julius? Tulip's alibis?

Shocked, Mr Barnes swings round to eavesdrop.

JULIUS How did you guess?

NATALIE Because I end up doing it myself. Practically every day now. But, Julius, she **couldn't** have done that stabbing. I've worked it out. It says that was at three, and we didn't finish with the school photo till ten minutes to. And Bridleford's **miles** away.

JULIUS That paper's full of foul stuff! Oh, Natty, surely there aren't that many horrid people in the world! And, if there are, I'm not sure I even want to go out any more, in case I meet them.

NATALIE There's horrid people in hotels, as well, you know. You're not safe here!

*Natalie 'comes to get him'. Cheered, **Julius** runs off. **Natalie** turns to find Mr Barnes staring.*

MR BARNES Listen, I know Tulip's turning into a bit of a bad lot, but this is ridiculous.

NATALIE Well, who **are** these people, if they're not people like her? *(fiercely)* And you knew, right from the start, it was likely to happen! That's why you never let me go round there. I heard you tell Mum it was 'no fit place for a child'. *(her voice is rising. Concerned staff and guests appear in doorways, watching)* And **Tulip** was a child. If you were so sure I shouldn't have been there, then she shouldn't have been there either!

MRS BARNES *stepping forward* Natalie, people can't go round snatching children from their parents just because those parents are awful.

NATALIE Why not? She shouldn't have been **left.**

MR BARNES People did **try,** you know. The schools tried. We made phone calls. So did other people. And there were social workers –

NATALIE *swinging round, furious, and seeing everyone* So **everyone** was in on it? You **all** knew? Well, what was the matter? *(sarcastically)* Wasn't it **bad** enough?

MR BARNES *crisply* No. It wasn't bad enough. And I'm afraid that life's a bit like that, Natalie. It has to be a whole lot worse than bad, to count as unbearable. And, till it gets to that point, people are on their own.

NATALIE *shouting sarcastically* Got to stick up for **themselves**, have they? However hard it is?

MR BARNES *shouting back* That's right. **You** managed it, didn't you? Look at you. No more warnings about report cards. No more lost hours after school. Better marks. Better habits. You dumped poor Tulip, and you've saved yourself.

Natalie goes ashen. Julius steps in to defend his sister.

JULIUS But Natalie's not like you, is she? She'd got no power to change things. Neither had I. Neither had Tulip. *(Julius points round the circle, indicting everyone)* But you lot had.

Natalie sinks to the floor, sobbing.

NATALIE Oh, Tulip! Tulip! I'm sorry. I'm so sorry!

Giving his parents a look sufficient to keep them away, Julius sinks beside his sister and puts his arms round her.

Scene Three

Christmas Eve in The Palace grounds. It's dark. Julius and Natalie are picking their way back towards the blinking Christmas lights of the hotel. Julius holds a bobbing torch. Natalie is wearing her father's Santa hat and carrying the rest of the costume. She is slightly tipsy.

NATALIE I don't see why he couldn't have thought to bring the costume in earlier. Hic! And I certainly don't see why **both** of us had to get frozen fetching it.

JULIUS That's because there's been a creeper.

NATALIE Sorry?

JULIUS A creeper. You know. Someone creeping about.

NATALIE How do you know? Hic!

JULIUS I heard Miss Ferguson telling Mrs Pettifer. 'Perverts' she kept saying. *(imitating)* 'I'd string them up, the whole lot of them.' And Mr Scott-Henderson told her it showed *(imitating)* 'an admirable, if somewhat unseasonal, spirit'.

NATALIE How does she know it's a pervert?

JULIUS I don't know. All George saw was somebody creeping about in the shadows. And someone broke in through the garage window.

NATALIE Hic! Do perverts like garages?

JULIUS How should I know what perverts like?

Natalie stumbles and ends up sitting on the lawn with her back to the blinking Palace lights.

NATALIE Whoops!

From this moment on, the blinking turns, almost imperceptibly, to flickering. And the sporadic faraway sounds of celebration are gradually overtaken by the sounds of crackling, spitting fire.

JULIUS Natalie! How much of that fizzy did Dad let you have?

NATALIE Just the one tiny glass...

JULIUS Ha!

NATALIE About this pervert –

JULIUS Oh, come on, Natty. I'm frozen. So someone's been creeping about, and breaking into garages, and spilling petrol –

NATALIE *suddenly sobering* Spilling petrol?

JULIUS So Chef said. He was furious. He was complaining all his toppings were picking up the smell. And Mr Stoddart said he slipped out for a quiet ciggie and dropped his match, and *(imitating)* 'half the bloody lawn went up! Scorched my best trousers!'.

NATALIE *urgently* Did he tell Dad?

Julius Of course not! You know what Mrs Stoddart's like. If she found out he'd taken up smoking again –

Natalie Julius! It's Tulip!

Julius Tulip?

Natalie *scrambling to her feet* Of course! *(they turn to look at the hotel, now clearly on fire. An alarm starts. There are faraway shouts of 'Fire!')* She **said** she'd pick the very best game of all. **And** that she'd win. And, look! Oh, clever, clever Tulip! To pick the one night everyone's in the same room, and all the staff are running round in circles, and everyone's too busy or too drunk to put two and two together. And everyone'll just think it's the Christmas lights – till it's too late. *(the fire is clearly out of control. We hear fire engine sirens. A megaphone telling people to gather at fire points)* Chef's *Boeuf* is definitely going to be *en croute* tonight!

Julius Natalie!

They convulse with laughter.

Natalie You had some too, didn't you? Admit it?

Julius Just a tiny glass. *(imitating her)* Hic!

Mr Barnes runs in.

Mr Barnes Is that you two? Thank God for that! Everyone else is out safely! I forbid you to come any nearer. Just stay here, safely, while your mother and I check the guest list. Natalie! Wrap yourself up in that Santa cloak at once. Stay warm. And keep together!

*Mr Barnes runs back. **Julius** and **Natalie** watch the fire. The colours flicker on their faces.*

Julius Not a pervert, then. An arsonist.

Natalie Poor Tulip. She'll be in such trouble now.

Julius Not with Mum and Dad, she won't.

Natalie What do you mean?

JULIUS I heard them talking. 'Our last Christmas' Dad was telling Mum. 'These grand old buildings have had their day. Too many planning rules. Hotels this size can't stay afloat with just a few loyal regulars and the odd passing tourist.'

NATALIE Were they going to move us?

JULIUS I guess. To one of those new places, maybe. You know. Fitness centre. Swimming pool. A proper dance floor.

NATALIE *dancing* Might be fun!

JULIUS Would you mind changing schools?

NATALIE I'd love it. Start again. How about you?

JULIUS I wouldn't mind.

NATALIE You wouldn't miss anyone?

JULIUS Not really. Not for long. Would you?

NATALIE Not really. *(pause)* Only Tulip.

JULIUS *admiringly* Look at that fire!

NATALIE How could she **do** that? How could she burn the only place she ever really loved to be?

JULIUS Does she care, do you think? Is she somewhere out here in the dark, do you think? Watching? *(**Tulip** appears silently behind them)* Remember the way she trailed her fingers up and down the bannisters as if she were a queen?

Tulip, as though young again, steps as though along a landing with her fingers resting lightly on bannisters.

NATALIE They'll be all charred and twisted now.

JULIUS And how she could never stop stroking the dimples in the bar top. Even after George had just finished polishing it.

Tulip fondly strokes an imaginary bar top.

NATALIE All that lovely dimpled copper. It'll have buckled and melted.

JULIUS Do you wish you'd never met her?

*Still unseen, **Tulip** waits in the shadows for the answer.*

NATALIE *forlornly* Oh, no. We had the best times **ever**.

JULIUS She'll have nothing in her life now. Except the police. And court cases. And endless horrid stuff like that.

NATALIE And everyone hating her for burning down a lovely old hotel.

JULIUS And bragging they all saw it coming. It's so mean of them! People like Tulip aren't locked doors. You can get through to them if you want.

NATALIE Do you think **I** could have stopped her?

JULIUS I don't know. Mrs Pettifer says there's no particular moment when someone goes to the bad. Each horrible thing that happens makes a difference. And there were probably too many of those in Tulip's life.

NATALIE You know, even the day I met her, she was going off to drown a kitten. But, then again, Dad was no older the day he pushed his grandfather's tortoise under the bush, and left it there to die. So you could say that Tulip was braver and kinder.

Tulip turns to go.

JULIUS I wonder what she's doing now.

NATALIE Crying her eyes out?

JULIUS Or laughing?

NATALIE Or not feeling anything, because feeling is just too painful.

JULIUS Or simply going home for one more beating, just for being late.

Tulip has gone.

NATALIE Poor Tulip.

JULIUS Poor Tulip.

NATALIE Poor Tulip.

Staging the Play

Aims

These activities will help you to:

- Understand the significance of the technical aspects of theatre
- Recognise the dramatic possibilities of the set, costume, sound and lighting
- Convey action and character in improvisation and performance
- Develop appropriate vocal and physical skills
- Evaluate your own work and that of others

How you choose to stage the play will depend on the resources available to you. If you have a large bare hall, you might think about staging it 'in the round', which means placing the audience on three or four sides of the acting area. If you have access to a theatre, you can present it in a traditional 'proscenium arch', where the audience looks into the dramatic world and between the audience and the stage is an invisible fourth wall. A 'thrust' stage means that the acting area extends beyond the proscenium arch and creates a more flexible acting area.

When you plan a performance of this play you'll need to be resourceful. What details might suggest 'a large faded country house hotel'? A couple of nice armchairs, a vase of flowers and a reception desk will help to create the atmosphere. Several scenes are set in the grounds. You might construct some moveable trellising, wound with fake plants, to act as a backdrop to these scenes. Different levels on the stage will break up the sightlines and create a more interesting dynamic. This will also serve as a way of showing distance or the relationship between characters. For example, Mrs Barnes, who is not an affectionate person, is first seen leaning over the bannisters, keeping her distance from her daughter.

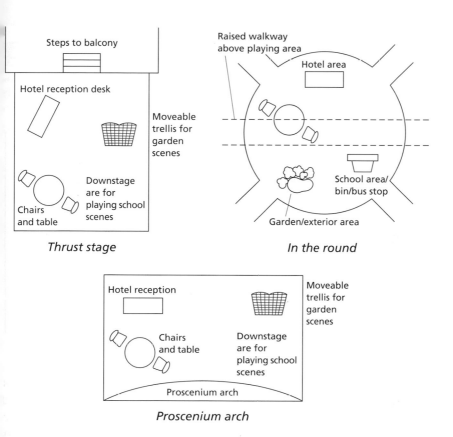

Thrust stage

In the round

Proscenium arch

LIGHTING

Lighting effects will help make the distinction between interior and exterior scenes. There are also several scenes set at or around school. It might be possible to place these at the front or side of the stage and leave the rest of the acting space in darkness.

Gobos, pieces of tin with shapes cut out, can be placed in front of the theatre lights to create dappled, leaf effects. The action takes place over the course of the year and lighting will help to suggest the passage of time. You could use fake candles and of course, fairy lights for the Christmas scenes and blue lighting to create a cold effect for outdoors. Again, gobos in front of red gel on the lights will add to the scene in which the fire happens. As this is the climax of the play the lighting at this point needs to be as dramatic as possible

PROPS

Read through the play carefully and make a list of any props that are mentioned. You may not be able to get hold of everything you need, so if resources are stretched decide which props are essential and which could be mimed. For example, the dressing up box is important because it gives Tulip an opportunity to show her acting skills. In another scene she admires herself in a mirror but she could simply show through her acting that she is looking in at her reflection.

It may be better to mime other vital props such as the kitten, the dead pigeon and the rabbit rather than representing them with soft toys. There is a danger that toys might make the scene amusing rather than sinister. Again, props can be a short cut for defining the age and status of various characters. Mr. Scott-Henderson could carry a copy of the *Daily Telegraph*, the teachers might be laden with files and books, and schoolchildren might carry rucksacks.

MUSIC AND SOUND EFFECTS

Music can be used to highlight the mood of a particular scene. Think of a particular tune or set of sounds that could be heard whenever Tulip appears. It might be more effective and subtle to create a sequence of sounds, for example a low percussion that gradually gets faster and accompanies each of Tulip's mad plans. Look for scenes where the dialogue has a rhythm to it and try simply clapping along as your actors go through the scene to see whether this works.

Think about current or recent pop songs that might be used to create an effect or make a point. Music is a good way to 'top and tail' scenes and provide a link during blackouts or scene changes. Make sure you choose music that fits with the atmosphere of the scene.

Appropriate sound effects will help create the atmosphere of key scenes, for example the fire. If you decide to use loud effects, make sure that your actors are still audible.

CASTING THE PLAY

In casting the play you need to think about the capabilities of the available actors. For example, the main characters of Natalie, Tulip and Julius are probably quite close to your own age. It can be difficult to find people who can take on roles that are older or younger than themselves. It is important to guard against caricature. Look up the definition of this word and work out how to make sure that the actors playing characters who may be older than their own parents or guardians, such as the sour Miss Ferguson, don't become caricatures. Stereotyping can happen when actors don't have much information or insight into the character. Try to avoid presenting a cliché of an old fussy person, and playing for laughs, rather than working to develop a fully rounded, believable person. Some of the exercises in the next section should help.

VOICE WORK

Think carefully about the way your character might speak. Mr. Scott-Henderson has, we can imagine, a posh, old-fashioned sort of voice, but what sort of voice would Tulip have? Would she have an accent? And would it be a country accent? Or a town accent? Would you make it slightly 'common' to mark out the social differences between herself and Natalie? Would it matter if they had the same sort of voice and accent? The person who plays Tulip will also have to work on developing her 'other' voice – the scary voice of her dad.

 Drama

In pairs

A. A says the sweetest loveliest things to B but in a really horrid, aggressive voice. B – says vicious, unpleasant things to A but in the nicest tone imaginable. This harder than it sounds! Swap over after a while. Listen to the effect of the contrast between tone and meaning. What do you notice? B must try to avoid sounding sarcastic.

On your own

B. Voices also need to be strong and audible. Breathing and vocal exercises will help. Take several slow deep breaths and make an 'oooo' sound on the out breath. Do this until you can really tune the volume up on the out breath and control the rate at which you release the breath. If you try to feel the sound coming from the pit of your stomach, you can make a huge sound with very little effort.

In pairs

C. One of you 'controls' the volume by raising or lowering their outstretched hand to 'conduct' the person making the sound. If you feel self-conscious making an open – vowel sound like an 'ahh' or 'ooo' then sing a note or hum or simply say your name. Swap places after while.

MOVEMENT

It is a good idea to do some stretching and movement exercises to help limber up at the start of each practical session, whether you intend to do some of the exercises or actually rehearse the play. This can also release any self-consciousness in improvising or performing.

 Drama

On your own

A. Crouch on the floor in your own space. Gradually grow and grow until you are fully extended and stretched upwards and on tiptoe. Hold the balance for a couple of breaths and then gradually, in a controlled way, collapse in on yourself, as if you are melting into the ground. Do this several times.

B. Move slowly and carefully around the room, gradually speeding up until you are running, being careful not to run into each other. Slow down gradually until you are moving in slow motion. Your teacher might want to give you the pace of this exercise by using a drum or other percussive instrument.

In pairs

C. Character movement. Think carefully about how your character might move, and how they walk and stand. In this exercise get into pairs, with one of you taking on the role of Natalie or Julius, depending on gender, and the other being either mum or dad. You are going to buy an ice cream from a van in the park. Walk and interact with your mum or dad on the way there as if you are the age of the character in the play, but as you are eating the ice cream you gradually become younger and younger until you are only five years old. How do you convey this from the way you move and speak? What can the person playing Natalie learn from this that will help her in the scene when Tulip first appears?

Work on and around the script

Aims

These activities will help you to:

- Explore and develop ideas, issues and relationships through work in role
- Develop dramatic techniques to enable you to create and sustain a variety of roles
- Analyse and discuss characters in a scene
- Consider different points of view
- Recognise and build on others' contributions
- Experiment with language to convey character and setting

THE CHARACTERS

 Character Profiles

If you are directing the play, you will need to ask everyone in the cast to write notes about the character they will play. This will mean going through the script very thoroughly to get clues about each character's background and motivation. We know a fair bit about Natalie and Tulip though not everything in their relationship is spelled out. It will be far more of a challenge to write notes for people like Mrs Pettifer or Mr. Scott-Henderson. Check how they respond to various situations in order, and this will help you to discover how they might have become the person they are. You'll need to use imagination as well as guesswork. Here is an example:

NAME: Susan Ferguson

AGE: 64

cont...

OCCUPATION: Senior civil servant at the Department of Transport, now retired.

HISTORY: Born in small seaside town. Lived with parents until they both died. Wanted to work abroad but was prevented by ill health. A long time ago fell in love with a married man. Very ashamed at how foolish she was but sometimes still misses him and feels lonely.

LIKES: Biographies and dachshunds

DISLIKES: Loud children

Emotional Maps – Discussion and Interpretation

Another way of helping to develop your character is to create an emotional map. This means placing your character in emotional relation to everyone else in the play so that you can demonstrate how close or far the characters are to each other. For example, Natalie's emotional map might look like this:

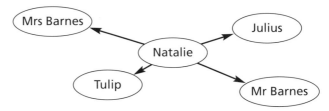

✎ Writing ☺ ☹

A. Create an emotional map like the one above for your character.

B. While you are comparing your emotional maps, take the opportunity to discuss the relationships in the play. We suspect that Mrs. Barnes seems to care more for Julius than she does for Natalie, but maybe she also cares more about the Hotel than her husband does. If this is your interpretation, the Hotel will be placed nearer to her on the emotional map. Maybe Tulip is only close to Natalie. How far away from her would you place Tulip's parents?

Bring your emotional maps to life by choosing different people to represent the various characters and their environments. For example, you might include Tulip's home, the Hotel and school. Each different placing of the characters in relation to the others and to key features of their environment will provide a different interpretation.

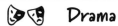 **Drama**

The following improvisations will help you to build a background for the characters in the play and create the atmosphere of the hotel.

A. CHECKING IN

In groups

Organisation: Work in several large groups. Everyone takes on a role as one of the characters in the play, another guest or a member of staff. Natalie and Julius might also become involved.

Situation: Every guest takes it in turn to check into the Hotel. Mr. and Mrs. Barnes welcome them and help them settle in. Can we learn anything about the family who own the Hotel while this is happening?

As each person interacts with other guests and the hotel staff, these are the kinds of questions that may come up:

- Have you ever stayed there before?
- Where have you come from?
- Why are you there?
- Do you know anyone else at the Hotel?

B. JOB INTERVIEWS

In groups

Organisation: Work in a group of three. Two of the group take on the roles of Mr. And Mrs. Barnes and the third is a potential cook, chambermaid or waiter.

Situation: Someone is applying for a specific position at the Hotel.

Preparation: Mr. and Mrs. Barnes prepare a list of questions to ask the potential employee.

The employee makes notes about the particular job that she or he is applying for, and invents some details of previous experience. In the improvisation it will be important to concentrate not just on the differences of the couple, but on their similarities. After all, they could hardly run a successful hotel if they weren't usually in agreement!

Opening line: Mrs Barnes: "You come highly recommended from your previous place of employment — the Grand Hotel. Why did you leave there, and why do you want to work at the Palace?"

cont...

Tableaux

Several times in the course of the play, Natalie speaks directly to the audience. The other characters must 'freeze' completely in order not to distract from what she is saying. This is known as creating a tableau or a still image. When this works well it means that even if lighting effects, such as a spotlight, aren't available then the attention of the audience will still be on Natalie.

 **Drama**

In groups of six to seven, pick different scenes from the play to present in tableau. For example, from the final section of the play these moments might be:

a   Tableau One – Christmas Day in the Hotel

b   Tableau Two – Someone smells burning

c   Tableau Three – Fire!

The scene where Tulip plays the practical joke on Jamie could be represented through tableaux. Again break the scene into three moments or tableaux. Share your work with other groups.

Best Friends

The friendship between Natalie and Tulip is a key relationship in the play and must be totally believable to the audience. The balance of power between the girls should be quite clear. How does this balance change during the course of the play? What is it that Natalie gets from her friendship with Tulip?

🎭 Drama

To help the actor playing Natalie, try the following improvisations:

A. *Organisation:* Work with a partner. One of you is Natalie and the other is Mrs. Barnes

Situation: Mrs Barnes trying to discourage Natalie from seeing Tulip

Opening Line: MRS. BARNES: "You're spending so much time with Tulip... I don't want your schoolwork to suffer."

B. *Organisation:* Work with a partner. One of you takes on the role of Natalie and the other is Julius.

Situation: Julius has heard about some of the practical jokes.

Opening Line: JULIUS: "It must be exciting to be Tulip's friend. Scary as well though...."

C. *Organisation:* Work in pairs. One is Natalie and the other is Mrs. Golightly

Situation: Mrs Golightly wants to separate the two friends.

Opening Line: NATALIE: "But you can't separate us, Mrs Golightly! Tulip is my friend!"

🗨️ Discussion

Is it important to have a best friend?
What should a best friend be like?
How would you expect a best friend to behave?
Write a description of your best friend.

Strange Insults

The insults that Tulip repeats are very strange and disturbing. They help to show us just how troubled her home life is. The author has Tulip's father go to some effort to create this effect through language. His words demonstrate the sort of person he is. He attacks his daughter with words as well as with physical abuse. Can you create some unusual and terrifying insults? Look at the examples from the play such as – "Snatch you bald-headed" or "Beat you like a red-headed step-child".

Creating insults

In groups

Organisation: Divide the class into three groups.

Tasks: Group A writes a list of verbs on separate pieces of paper;
Group B makes a list of nouns;
Group C writes down a list of adjectives.

These do not need to be deliberately scary words. The language used in the play is a mixture of ordinary and extra-ordinary words and phrases and it is this mixture that makes it so effective.

Each group takes random selections of words from the other groups to create threatening phrases and sentences. These phrases should be the beginnings of the kind of scary language that Tulip's dad might use.

Development:
Work in small groups. Each group takes a phrase, and works out a story behind it. For example, you might invent a story from which the phrase 'snatch you bald-headed' might have come. It might be about a naughty child who pulls his classmates' hair for a joke until one day his own hair is torn clean off by a giant eagle. Look at myths and fairy stories and legends for inspiration for your own stories.

ALTERNATIVE ENDINGS

Discussion and Writing

Is there a moment in the play when things might have turned out differently for Tulip? Could she and Natalie have remained friends? Mr. Barnes was always very sympathetic towards her. Could he have taken steps to help her? Who might have been on her side?

Write a new ending for the play in the form of:

a A final scene which shows us Tulip being given a chance for a new life
Or:
b A letter from Tulip, now aged 25, to Natalie, in which she describes what happened to her after the Barnes family moved away from the Hotel
Or:
c Improvise a meeting between Tulip and Natalie, who are now both grown up, in which they share the details of their lives since the fire.

From Novel to Playscript

Aims

These activities will help you to:

- Identify the main ideas in a text
- Use stylistic conventions
- Explore how form contributes to meaning
- Identify the ways implied and explicit meanings are conveyed

---

In the novel, *The Tulip Touch*, author Anne Fine includes several scenes that don't appear in the play. In turning the novel into a play, she has made numerous changes. For example, in the novel Julius is just a baby, but in the play he is just a few years younger than Natalie. The reason for this is that the author wanted to have someone for Natalie to confide in. In a novel the character's thoughts can be confided directly to the reader, and although in a play characters can tell us their thoughts through what is known as a soliloquy, if it is overused this technique can have a negative effect and slow down the drama. The scenes between Natalie and Julius tell us more about Tulip and what people think of her, as well as about the friendship between Tulip and Natalie.

The author never brings Tulip's father on stage. Why do you think this is? What is gained by leaving this character to our imaginations?

Look at the following extract from the book *The Tulip Touch*. Working in groups of four, decide who will be the director and who will play the different characters in the scene.

And there's another time I shan't forget, when I cut my knee, wading over to the stone boy in the lily pond. I was carrying a hat we had spent hours dressing with feathers, so I didn't dare use my hands to save myself when I stumbled and fell against the sharp side of his pedestal.

Blood poured from the gash. I looked down and felt quite frightened. With each step I took against the water, blood washed away, then welled again.

'Hurry!' yelled Tulip. 'Walk faster! Run!'

No one can run through water. By the time I got to the edge, my heart was thumping. Tulip prised the hat from my hands. It wasn't even splashed.

'Good heavens, child!'

One of the guests had strolled over to see what was happening. Scattering peacocks, she hurried me up the terrace and propped me against a ledge. First came a linen cloth from one of the bars. I soaked that scarlet in seconds. Then came the towels. And then my parents arrived.

Tulip danced round, getting in everyone's way as Dad went to fetch a car as close as he could without flattening the flower beds, and everyone else spilled out advice.

'You realize she'll need at least half a dozen stitches.'

'I shouldn't bother with the surgery. I'd take her straight to Casualty at the hospital.'

'Don't worry, Mrs. Barnes. These things so often look a whole lot worse than they are.'

Dad appeared round the corner. Behind him, a car engine throbbed. I was handed down over the terrace, and Mum ran to keep up as Dad strode with me in his arms towards the back seat. He tipped me in, and Mum threw herself in beside me and slammed the door after her.

Someone opened the door again, to push in more towels.

'Oh, thank you!' said Mum. 'Thank you!'

I heard a sharp tap, and looked through the other window. Tulip was just outside, prancing about like a monkey. She made a stupid face, splaying her hands, tipping her head sideways and sticking out her tongue.

Turning away, I caught the look my mother gave her in return. I shut my eyes then. I can shut them now. But I can still see both their faces.

Tulip's? Well, ugly and uncaring, certainly.

But Mum's?

Far, far more disturbing, somehow. I can't really explain. All I can tell you is that Mum was looking at Tulip the way no one normally looks at a child.

---

෬ ෭ Discussion

- Work out how you will stage the scene.
- What dialogue will you need to change or leave out?
- What do you think is the dramatic climax to the scene?
- How can you intensify this moment?
- Write out your dramatised version of this incident in play format, complete with stage directions.
- Present your version of the scene to others in the class.

✍ Writing a Review

Once you have performed *The Tulip Touch*, you could try writing a review. Aim for about 250 words and think about how to convey the action on the stage to your readers. You should also consider what you want to say about the production. What were the performances like? What did you think of the set, the lighting, costumes? Was it overall an effective production of the play? Justify your opinion. If you feel you are too close to the play to write a really objective review, you could choose to write a review of a film or TV programme you've seen recently. What are the main skills needed to be an effective reviewer?

✍ Rewriting a Review

Read the following review of Anne Fine's novel *The Tulip Touch*.

***

There's not much comedy this time in Fine's disturbing story, only the nervous laughter evoked by cruel insults and spiteful tricks. With thrilling intensity, she dramatizes the attraction the good girl feels for the dangerous outsider. The narrator, Natalie, feels safe in her loving home, which is a country mansion hotel, where her gentle father is the manager. He forbids her to go to her classmate Tulip's home, a shack dominated by Tulip's abusive, terrifying dad; but Tulip is welcome at the hotel, and the girls become inseparable at school. Spellbound, Natalie

cont...

watches Tulip run wild. Then, gradually, Natalie joins in the troublemaking, giving up her drab, nondescript self to cry "Havoc!" She is at once pitying, scared, disgusted, and enthralled. With huge effort, she finally breaks free and saves herself ("It was like coming out of the hospital") but only by destroying Tulip, who then spirals totally out of control and brings everything crashing down. Even in her funniest stories, such as *Flour Babies* (1994), Fine is didactic; here the moralizing is direct (What chance did Tulip have in her desolate home? Why didn't anyone help her?), but the message grows right out of an action-packed story that not only humanizes the bully but also reveals the ugly secrets of the respectable. (Why do we enjoy watching a building in flames? Who is guilty? What is evil?) The plush hotel setting with its bored guests is a perfect backdrop, and readers will be as excited as Natalie by the wild, subversive invader. They will swallow this book in one gulp, and then they might want to talk about it and go on to read Cynthia Voigt's funny *Bad Girls* (1996) and, for older readers, Margaret Atwood's adult novel *Cat's Eye* (1989).

Hazel Rochman
(Booklist/September 15, 1997)

Do you agree with this review? Could you re-write it in simpler language for a younger audience?

Themes in and around the play

Aims

These activities will help you to:

- Explore and develop ideas, issues and relationships through work in role
- Take different roles in discussion
- Organise and present information
- Select appropriate material
- Give written advice
- Investigate the different ways familiar themes are explored by different writers
- Experiment with presenting material in different forms for different audiences

THE ORIGINS OF EVIL

ඩ‍෫ ඥ‍ Discussion

Several people in the play describe Tulip as evil, although Mr. Barnes claims that there's no such thing. Do you think Tulip is evil? What is the dictionary definition of evil? Do you agree? Take a couple of tabloid newspapers and look at how often this word is used. Is it used in the correct way? Is describing someone as evil a convenient way of not, as a society, taking responsibility for them? Is evil learnt or do you think one can be born evil?

✎ Writing a Report

Write a social worker's report on Tulip. The report should focus on her situation and try and analyse what is happening. Use the following headings to guide you.

Report

Name: Tulip Pierce

Age: 13

Home: A description of Tulip's house and its contents, including anything that might seem odd or out of place.

Parents: Are they happy to be interviewed? What are their responses to the questions the social worker asks? What is their attitude to Tulip's schoolwork and behaviour?

Teachers: What are their attitudes to Tulip? Are any of the teachers prepared to help the social worker with information or insight into Tulip?

Tulip: Does she feel anxious, neglected or angry? What would she like to happen in an ideal world? Does she worry about the future?

🎭 Role Play

In order to help with this report, the whole group takes on different roles. One person in role as the social worker interviews them.

In pairs

A. *Organisation:* Work in pairs in role as Mrs Pierce and Chris George, the social worker.

Situation: Chris wants to interview them at their home. He rings for an appointment and speaks to Mrs. Pierce.

Opening line: MRS PIERCE: You could come round Thursday. I know he won't be here then. CHRIS: But it's important I see both of you, Mrs. Pierce".

In groups

B. *Organisation:* Work in threes, in role as Chris and Mr. and Mrs. Pierce at their home.

Situation: Chris is keen to get as much background information on Tulip as she can and her parents are the best people to help with this.

Opening line: CHRIS: I thought it would be a good opportunity for us to meet without Tulip around."

cont...

In pairs

C. Organisation: Work in pairs, in role as Chris and Mrs. Golightly.

Situation: Chris needs to interview Mrs. Golightly about Tulip and her schoolwork.

Opening line: CHRIS: I understand that Tulip doesn't take school very seriously. How long has this been going on?

D. Organisation: Work in pairs, in role as Chris and Natalie.

Situation: Chris wants to know as much as possible about the games that Natalie and Tulip play.

Opening line: CHRIS: I see, so Days of Dumbness was a way of annoying other people. Did all Tulip's games end up with you both annoying other people?

 ## Law and Order

As a class

Imagine that Tulip has been charged with starting the fire at the Hotel. What would happen to her at the hearing? Would she have someone to defend her? What witnesses would be called? You could use the work you've done in the role-play exercises above to build up a courtroom scene.

You will need to include Mr. and Mrs. Barnes as well as the testimony of the social worker and the policemen who were investigating the incident of Muriel Brackenbury. Choose several people to play the magistrate, Tulip's lawyer and any other extra characters that may be needed.

Find out how a Youth Court operates. Make sure that the correct language is used and that formal procedures are observed. If anyone breaks the rules and is found in contempt of court, then they can be evicted.

Think about the following:

How will you set up your space to resemble a courtroom?
Will her parents be called to give evidence? Remember that evidence can be used either to support the charge of arson or to deny it. Maybe Tulip has an alibi. Maybe the social workers report will convince the magistrate that she had such a bad start in life she should be given another chance. Decide the structure of what happens.

✍ Writing

A. THE DIARY

Imagine Tulip keeps a diary. Try to write entries from her diary that deal with significant moments in her life. For example there might be an entry after her first meeting with Natalie which would mention the kitten and this girl who doesn't know her but wants to be her friend. Another entry might be about the Christmas Day she spends with the Barnes's at the Hotel.

B. THE LETTER

Natalie feels guilty about dropping Tulip. Try writing a letter from Natalie to Tulip explaining why she's abandoned her and how she feels about it.

Starting point:

"I know you may never answer this letter. And I wouldn't blame you. I just started to feel that I had started to change...maybe it's growing up or something...but you hadn't. Or at least not in a way that made me want to be with you...."

C. THE NEWSPAPER REPORT

Imagine you are a newspaper reporter who has been sent to cover the fire at the hotel for a front page article. Before beginning writing, you might first role-play interviews with Hotel guests and staff who witnessed the fire. How much can the reporter find out by interviewing them? What is the most interesting aspect of the story? Do the police know who did it? Are they revealing all they know? The reporter can also interview the officer in charge of the investigation. Maybe there is a follow up story the reporter can write once the culprit – Tulip –has been caught.

Things to think about:

What sort of newspaper are you writing for?

Is it a tabloid or a broadsheet?

What differences would this make to the language you use and to the aspects of the story that you chose to emphasise?

cont...

LOCAL HOTEL BURNS DOWN; GIRL SUSPECTED

Luxury hotel in mysterious fire. Police suspect arson

WILD CHILD LOVES PLAYING WITH FIRE, SAY VICTIMS OF HOTEL BLAZE

Pick one of the above headlines and continue your report in the same style.

FRIENDSHIP AND BULLYING

Friendship is one of the central themes in the book. It explores the nature of friendship and when friendship tips over into being exploitative or bullying.

⟨₃ ₃⟩ Discussion ✎

Write a list of words that summarise the meaning of friendship. As a whole class, you might brainstorm your ideas and create a single list, or you could choose to work separately and share your ideas when you've finished.

Next, write a list of words that come to mind when you hear the word 'bully'. Do any of these words fit the character of Tulip as you understand it from the play?

Read this extract from the novel *Cat's Eye* by the Canadian writer Margaret Atwood. Elaine, the narrator describes a childhood memory.

We've forgotten the time, it's getting dark. We run along the street that leads to the wooded footbridge. Even Grace runs, lumpily, calling 'Wait up!' For once she is the one left behind.

Cordelia reaches the hill first and runs down it. She tries to slide, but the snow is too soft, not icy enough, and there were cinders and pieces of gravel in it. She falls down and rolls. We think she's done it on purpose, the way she made the snow angel. We rush down upon her, exhilarated, breathless, laughing, just as she's picking herself up.

We stop laughing, because now we can see that her fall was an accident, she didn't do it on purpose. She likes everything she does to be done on purpose.

Carol says, 'Did you hurt yourself?' Her voice is quavery, she's frightened, already she can tell that this is serious. Cordelia doesn't answer. Her face is hard again, her eyes baleful.

Grace moves so that she's beside Cordelia, slightly behind. From there she smiles at me, her tight smile.

Cordelia says to me, 'Were you laughing?' I think she means, was I laughing at her because she fell down.

'No,' I say.

'She was,' says Grace neutrally. Carol shifts to the side of the path, away from me.

'I'm going to give you one more chance,' says Cordelia. 'Were you laughing?'

'Yes,' I say, 'but….'

'Just yes or no,' says Cordelia.

I say nothing. Cordelia glances over at Grace, as if looking for approval. She sighs, an exaggerated sigh, like a grown-ups.

'Lying again,' she says. 'What are we going to do with you?'

We seem to have been standing there for a long time. It's colder now. Cordelia reaches out an pulls off my knitted hat. She marches the rest of the way down the hill and onto the bridge and hesitates for a moment. Then she walks over to the railing and throws my hat down into the ravine. Then the white oval of her face turns up towards me. 'Come here,' she says.

Nothing has changed, then. Time will go on, in the same way, endlessly. My laughter was unreal after all, merely a gasp for air.

I walk down to where Cordelia stands by the railing, the snow not crunching but giving way under my feet like cotton-wool packing. It sounds like a cavity being filled, in a tooth, inside my head. Usually I'm afraid to go so near the edge of the bridge, but this time I'm not. I don't feel anything as positive as fear.

'There's your stupid hat,' says Cordelia; and there it is, far down, still blue against the white snow, even in the dimming light. 'Why don't you go down and get it?'

I look at her. She wants me to go down into the ravine where the bad men are, where we're never supposed to go. It occurs to me that I may not. What will she do then?

I can see this idea gathering in Cordelia as well. Maybe she's gone too far, hit, finally, some core of resistance in me. If I refuse to do what she says this time, who knows where my defiance will end? The two others have come down the hill and are watching, safely in the middle of the bridge.

'Go on then,' she says, more gently, as if she's encouraging me, not ordering. 'Then you'll be forgiven.'

I don't want to go down there. It's forbidden and dangerous; also it's dark and the hillside will be slippery, I might have trouble climbing up again. But there is my hat. If I go home without it, I'll have to explain, I'll have to tell. And if I refuse to go, what will Cordelia do next? She might get angry, she might never speak to me again. She might push me off the bridge. She's never done anything like that before, never hit or pinched, but now that she's thrown my hat over, there's no telling what she might do.

I walk along to the end of the bridge. 'When you've got it, count to a hundred,' says Cordelia. 'Before coming up.' She doesn't sound like someone giving instructions for a game.

I start down the steep hillside, holding on to branches and tree trunks. The path isn't even a real path, it's just a place worn by whoever goes up and down here: boys, men. Not girls.

Script Writing

In groups

Organisation: Work in groups of three, and recreate the two scenes. You might want to write a script first and add dialogue or narration if you feel it is needed. This might, for example, tell your audience how deep the ravine is and how cold the weather is. Share your work with everyone else.

🎭 Drama

In pairs

A. *Situation:* Elaine's mother questions her about her friendship with Cordelia. How much does Elaine tell her of what actually happened at the ravine?

Opening line: MOTHER: But you used to be such great friends and all of a sudden you don't seem to be interested in seeing her...

In groups

B. *Organisation:* Work in groups of three.

Situation: Cordelia is trying to recruit a new 'friend'. Elaine overhears and tries to intervene.

Opening lines: CORDELIA: I think we'll get along really well. You can come to mine and play whenever you like. You want to watch out for Elaine. She isn't very loyal.

Presenting Information

A. What policies does your school have on bullying? Get a copy of these, and, working on your own, re-write them as if they are meant for a primary school. You will need to consider the following:

What changes will you need to make in the language?

Is there a better way of communicating the rules and procedures for dealing with bullying?

Is it possible to stop bullying before it becomes a serious problem?

In groups

B. Working in small groups, design anti-bullying posters. Come together as a group and decide which of your posters work best and why.

C. Using the posters as a starting point, create a TV advertisement aimed at preventing bullying. You have to decide as a group what are the main causes of bullying. In Tulip's case, it is because she has an unhappy background but is this true for every bully? Is it because bullies feel insecure and would rather have any kind of attention than none at all? Do they get a thrill out of making people frightened of them? Most bullies 'grow out of it' eventually. Why?

Your TV ad should be no longer that 60 seconds so think carefully about which images will work best and how to make the script clear and succinct. Would you include an anti-bullying rap or a song to go with it? If you had unlimited resources what would you add to your commercial to make it stronger?

TRUTH AND LIES

Discussion

In groups

A. Tulip is an expert liar. Do you think that lying can ever be justified?

Think of some famous liars. Maybe you can name some recent politicians or celebrities who have lied publicly. Or maybe you can remember some recent plot lines in soap operas that rely on someone being evasive or concealing information.

cont...

B. Liars could be put into three different categories. Those who lie to punish people and make them feel bad, those who lie to protect themselves and those who lie for self-promotion.

Make a list of people who have lied, either real or from literature or TV.

Work in small groups and come up with examples of liars who fit into each category. Share your work with the rest of the group. Do you all agree?

۞ ۞ Debate

Organise a class debate entitled:

'Lying is sometimes justified' versus 'Lying is never right'. To make it interesting, ask for a show of hands for each argument and then swap the debaters over, so people have to argue for the statement they don't necessarily agree with.

Billy Liar

Billy Liar is a comedy about a boy who tells lies and uses fantasy to escape from his dull existence. He has become simultaneously engaged to two girls, Barbara and Rita, and is hoping to avoid the problem by leaving home. His dream is to go to London and become a scriptwriter. In this scene, Barbara has come to tea and witnessed a quarrel between Billy and his father, during which Billy's grandmother has been taken ill.

Read the extract and decide which category of liar Billy falls into.

BARBARA Do you think she'll be all right – your grandmother?

BILLY Who? Oh, my grandma! Yes, she'll be all right. It's just that she's got this rare disease – they're trying a new drug out on her.

BARBARA She looked as though she was having some kind of fit at first. I noticed when you were having that row with your father.

BILLY They've only tried it out three times – this drug. Once on President Eisenhower, then the Duke of Windsor and then my grandma.

BARBARA Honestly! No wonder your father gets cross with you.

BILLY How do you mean?

BARBARA Well, all these stories you keep on telling – no wonder he keeps losing his temper.

BILLY Oh, you don't take any notice of him.

BARBARA Billy?

BILLY What?

BARBARA What was your father saying? About you going to London?

BILLY Did he? When? I never heard him.

BARBARA When he was talking about answering back at your grandmother. When he got hold of your shirt, He said, "If you want to go to London you can 'B' well go." He swore.

BILLY I know. He's been summonsed twice for using bad language.

BARBARA Yes, but what did he mean?

BILLY What? About going to London?

BARBARA Yes.

BILLY Ah, well – there's a very interesting story behind that.

BARBARA No, Billy, this is important – to us. You've got to think about me now.

BILLY *(rising and crossing towards her)* It's for you I'm doing it, my darling.

BARBARA What do you mean?

BILLY *(sitting down beside her and taking her hand, he goes off into a fantasy)* Isn't it obvious? How can we go on living like this?

BARBARA *(automatically freeing her hand, she takes an orange from her handbag)* What do you mean, pet? Like what?

BILLY In this – this atmosphere. Do you honestly think that we could ever be happy – I mean really happy – here?

BARBARA Where?

BILLY In this house. There's the shadow of my father across this house. He's a bitter man, Barbara.

BARBARA *(settling down and beginning to peel the orange)* Why? What for? What about?

BILLY He's jealous. Every time he looks at me he sees his own hopes and the failure of his own ambitions.

BARBARA Your father?

BILLY He had his dreams once. He can't bear it – seeing me on the brink of success. He was going to be a writer too.

BARBARA Billy, if this is going to be another of your stories.....

BILLY You don't have to believe me. The evidence is here – in this house.

BARBARA Evidence? How do you mean – evidence?

BILLY *(pointing to the sideboard)* It's all in there.

BARBARA What is?

BILLY Go and look for yourself. In that cupboard.

(Barbara rises and crosses to the sideboard. She tugs at the handle on Billy's cupboard)

BARBARA It's locked.

BILLY *(meaningly)* Yes.

BARBARA Where's the key?

BILLY God knows. I was four years old when that was locked, Barbara. It's never been opened since.

BARBARA *(crossing towards Billy)* Well, what's supposed to be in it?

BILLY Hopes! Dreams! Ambitions! The life work of a disillusioned man. Barbara, there must be forty or fifty unpublished novels in that cupboard. All on the same bitter theme.

BARBARA *(in half-belief)* Well, we can't all be geniuses.

BILLY Perhaps not. But he crucified himself in the attempt. Sitting night after night at that table. Chewing at his pen. And when the words wouldn't come he's take it out on us.

BARBARA But what about going to London? What about our cottage in Devon?

BILLY Well, it's all down south, Barbara. We could live in the New Forest. We could have a cottage there – a woodman's cottage – in a clearing.

BARBARA I think I'd be frightened. Living in a forest.

BILLY Not with me to look after you, you wouldn't.

(From *Billy Liar* by Keith Waterhouse and Willis Hall. Published by Samuel French Ltd.)

Discussion

- Would you call Billy's fantasies 'lies' or 'stories', as Barbara calls them?
- Which of his 'stories' is Barbara inclined to believe in?
- What kinds of fantasy do you think Barbara engages in?
- What impression do we get of his home life and his relationship with his father?
- What do you think might actually be in the locked sideboard?
- Does Billy use any 'Tulip touches' in his fantasies?
- Does Billy's behaviour remind you of the way Tulip behaves?

GENDER DIVISION

Would it have been possible for Anne Fine to have written this play with two boys as the main characters? What changes would she have had to make? Would the plot be different? Would boys play the sort of 'acting' games that Natalie and Tulip play? Would they have had a physical fight at some point or been aggressive to people from school?

 **Drama**

Look at these two scenes from the play

1. **DOG POO SCENE**

   How would you re-work this scene for boys to play? Would you swap the gender of the recipient as well? Would the incident be more likely to turn into a fight if all the protagonists were male?

   29–30

2. **RABBIT SCENE**

   In pairs, improvise around these scenes but using two boys. What changes will you make? Present your work to the rest of the group. How does your audience respond? Is the scene as believable? If not, why not? Is it because we don't think boys are as badly affected by abuse? Are they expected to cope with it better?

   35–37

ARSON

Arson becoming a Devastating National Crime in the USA

Source: *Western Insurance Information Services*

Arson kills more than 700 people, destroys over 100,000 buildings and costs more than $2 billion each year. Surprisingly, children are the cause of half of all arson fires in this country.

Some statistics on Kids and Fire:

- Curiosity is the most common reason children play with fire;
- 49% of those arrested for arson are juveniles;
- More than 300 people die in residential fire each year as a result of children playing with fire;
- Fires started by children represent 3 out of 10 pre-school deaths;
- Each year, more than 28,000 residential fires are caused by children playing with fire.

Smoke Signals: Recognising Fire and Arson Behaviour in Children

Children (under 6 years old) – "Curiosity Fire Setters"
Signs to look for include playing with matches or lighters, burned toys, attraction to fire and spent matches.

Children (6–12 years) – "Recurrent Fire Setters"
Signs to look for include concealment of matches and lighters, excitement at fires, temper outbursts and destructive or physically violent behaviour.

Adolescent Fire Setters – "Pathological Fire Setters and Arsonists"
Signs to look for include power struggles with adults, desire to be a hero, lack of empathy with others, sexual confusion and conflict, and rebellious, oppositional and defiant attitudes.

Smoke Signals: Recognising Environmental Changes that May Lead to Arson Behaviour.

- Recent changes in the child's family structure, such as divorce, separation, new baby or death of a relative;
- Child has been under severe stress in the past six months, such as move to another neighbourhood or loss of friends;
- Fighting between child and parents or siblings increases markedly;
- Child believes that fire can do magical things;
- Child dreams about fire at night or talks about fire during the day.

We pay for arson. We pay for it in higher property insurance premiums and in higher taxes. We also pay in costs that can't be measured in dollars…in hundreds of lives lost each year…in thousands of arson survivors who end up physically or emotionally scarred…in what once were homes or thriving businesses…in added fear of crime.

Are there any clues in this extract to Tulip's fascination with fire? Which category does she fit into?

> ③✎ **Presenting Information**
>
> Read the extract carefully and select what you feel are the most significant facts. Make a formal two-minute presentation about the dangers of arson, aimed at parents and teachers. Be prepared to answer any questions your audience may have about the material in your speech.

> ✍ **Writing**
>
> Write a story about a child who fits one of the descriptions above. What motivates the main character to light fires? Is there a sad or a happy ending to your story?

CHILD ABUSE

At the end of the play, Natalie is furious because everyone, including herself, has abandoned Tulip. What action has been taken to help Tulip? Why does her father get away with his treatment of her?

Read the following extract from *The Orchard on Fire* by Sheena Mackay:

'What happened when you got back last night?' I asked Ruby on the way to school. I was wearing my pixie-hood. I was going to tell Miss Fay I had earache and ask if I could keep it on in class.

'Nothing. Your dad marched straight up to the bar and said to my dad, 'What do you mean by treating your daughter like that? You're nothing but a bully and a coward. And letting her run round the village in the dark!' I thought my dad was going to hit him but my mum goes, 'I was just putting on my coat to look for her. Ruby, you naughty girl, sneaking out when you're supposed to be in bed,' and then she tells your dad that I cut off my hair myself in a fit of temper. 'What fibs has she been telling you?' she goes, and your dad goes, 'I believe what Ruby told me.' Everybody's staring, Mr. Vinnegar and Sack and Mr. Annett and some other people.

Then my dad says, 'Get up to bed Ruby. I'll deal with you in the morning. Thanks for bringing her home anyway,' and my mum goes, 'Have a drink, Mr. Harlency, on the house,' and your dad goes, 'I'm a bit choosy who I drink with. If you so much as lay a finger on that child again I'll knock your teeth down your flaming throat.'

'Blimey. Good old Percy; what happened next?'

'Your dad walked out and my dad came upstairs and belted me one.' Then she said, scuffing her shoe on the pavement, 'I'm not allowed to come round your house any more, and you're not allowed to come to tea on my birthday'.

From *The Orchard on Fire* by Sheena Mackay, published by
Vintage UK, Random House

This is a similar situation to the one that Tulip is in. The father takes action by threatening Ruby's father. Does this have any effect? Should people take the law into their own hands?

☺☺ Discussion

Have a debate about vigilantes. Have there been any real life examples or situations in soap operas where there have been instances of vigilante action recently? If so, what have been the outcomes? Is there a danger that the laws of the land get disregarded in the emotion of ordinary people 'punishing' those who abuse children? Is it acceptable to take action if the law doesn't seem to be protecting the most vulnerable members of society? Why are some men violent towards their wives or children? Why do some women hit their husbands or boyfriends or children?

Read the following extract from *Once in House on Fire* by Andrea Ashworth

---

'We were meaning it as a surprise, Dad,' I said. 'Mum didn't know.'

'Shut it,' he said.' And don't you be defending this slag – she's a bad mother, she is, lazing on her arse when she should be up and cooking.'

Our mother stiffened her shoulders. 'That's bloody evil,' she gritted. 'What've you done for them lately, you greedy sod, except guzzle the food money so's I can't feed them like I should?'

He lunged to slap her.

'Cheeky bitch!' He missed her face, but tore the silver butterfly out of our mother's lobe.

She winced and put her hand over the rip.

'Get to your bedroom, girls.' She spoke without looking at us, eyes fixed on our stepfather.

They stood facing one another, anger simmering in each of their faces, like a mirror.

Our mother was flaming livid. Our stepfather was flaming livid.

'Get to your bedroom,' she said again, in a strange mannish voice.

Thinking of punches and slaps and the beef-knife flashing in our mother's face, my stomach churned to leave them alone.

My voice cracked when I dared, 'But we've not eaten yet.'

'Get into your room and lock the door!' Our mother screamed when our stepfather grabbed the pan of boiling macaroni off the stove, swinging around to face her. I stood frozen, gripping Laurie and Sarah by the hands, until my mother shoved me.

'Get to your room. Call Auntie Penney, then lock the door,' she said.

We stood our ground. The pan was bubbling and spotting in his fist. Our mother looked naked in the face of it.

'No, Mum,' I found myself crying, 'Please, Dad, you're frightening us.'

Laurie and Sarah took on my tears: we had all three of us seen our mother's face smacked scarlet, punched purple-blue, but the water was something else.

Simmering. Scalding.

Our stepfather looked at us, then turned away.

'Oh, Jesus!' He flung the boiling water and macaroni behind him into the window, letting the pan clang into the sink. Pasta slithered slowly down the pane and over the sill.

'Christ, what am I doing?' Our stepfather grabbed his hair in his fists and scrunched his face tight red. His eyes were wet slits. He opened them and looked at us all, crying.

'I'm sorry. Jesus, I'm sorry.'

From *Once in House on Fire* by Andrea Ashworth, Picador

---

෬෭ Discussion

What does the author reveal about the family? Why do families protect the abuser? And how do they do it? Whose fault is it that this abuse happens? Is it possible to break the cycle of abuse? Families are often financially dependent on the man in house. Is this a powerful reason not to tell the police or anyone else what is going on?

Research resources and further reading

Agencies:

Childline – a free confidential 24-hour phone service for children or young people in trouble or danger — 0800 1111

www.childline.co.uk

Further reading:

The Book of the Banshee by Anne Fine – Collins Educational, 1995

A Child called It by David Selzer

Cat's Eye by Margaret Atwood

Once in House on Fire by Andrea Ashworth, Picador

The Orchard on Fire by Sheena Mackay, Vintage UK, Random House

The Bully by Jan Needle – Collins Educational, 2000

Web resources:

www.annefine.co.uk